FOUR FOR FOGO ISLAND

Kevin Major

For their altruism and goodwill, the author extends his gratitude to the people he came to know on Fogo Island and Change Islands. To editors Marnie Parsons and Claire Wilkshire, and all the team at Breakwater Books, he sends huge thanks for their dedication, attention to detail, and generous spirit.

BREAKWATER
P.O. Box 2188, St. John's, NL, Canada, A1C 6E6
WWW.BREAKWATERBOOKS.COM

A CIP CATALOGUE RECORD FOR THIS BOOK IS AVAILABLE FROM LIBRARY AND ARCHIVES CANADA.

COPYRIGHT © 2022 Kevin Major
ISBN 978-1-55081-952-6

Cover photograph by Linda Osmond | Herring Cove Art Gallery & Studio, Fogo Island, NL

We acknowledge the support of the Canada Council for the Arts. We acknowledge the financial support of the Government of Canada and the Government of Newfoundland and Labrador through the Department of Tourism, Culture, Arts and Recreation for our publishing activities.
PRINTED AND BOUND IN CANADA.

 Canada Council Conseil des Arts
for the Arts du Canada

Canada Newfoundland Labrador

Breakwater Books is committed to choosing papers and materials for our books that help to protect our environment. To this end, this book is printed on a recycled paper that is certified by the Forest Stewardship Council®.

perfect points to you, my family of quilters

On her quilting table is a small, elegant pair of scissors, cast in the shape of a stork, a design that dates back to eighteenth-century Europe. The bird's body is plated with gold, and the wings with nickel, as is the narrow, elongated beak. When opened, the beak forms a pair of knife-edged blades. When closed, they taper to a very fine, very sharp point.

She loves the elegance that the stork scissors bring to her routine. She uses them by day to snip threads as she sews the choice cotton fabrics that make up her quilts, and in the evenings, if she is embellishing sections, she uses them to cut strands of embroidery floss.

In her hand the scissors are a charmed accompaniment to the needlework traditions of her island home.

But in the hand of her murderer they puncture the carotid artery in her neck, causing her to hemorrhage and die within minutes.

Such is the irony of the small, treasured crafting tool that had been handed down from her grandmother to her mother to her. An implement for delicate stitchery, but equally a weapon as deadly as any lancet or dagger.

The woman fell to the floor, where she was soon surrounded by a splay of blood. Her murderer covered her with a half-finished quilt, its pattern the Lover's Knot.

DOUBLE IRISH CHAIN

WHAT A DIFFERENCE a Mae makes.

To be honest, I wasn't expecting it. Then again, being middle-aged and re-singled, I had yet to figure out just what to expect. Surprise is always good. I take the surge of relationship adrenaline as an alert to the fact that the best years might yet be ahead of me. Hah.

I've upped my clothes game, and in the hair department I've ditched the long-standing side part for something short and slightly spiky. I've initiated a brief but intense home-exercise workout to tighten the upper body.

The renewed me. Dog Gaffer is impressed. As for son Nick, let the tyranny begin.

'Whoa. The dude has done the job on himself.' This after a first glance, before he even has his jacket off.

'Whataya think?'

'Different.'

'C'mon, you can do better than that.'

Nick picks up the excited Gaffer and stands closer for a more thorough inspection. I'm still getting used to the fact that our eyes are almost level. At sixteen, he has an inch to go to the big 6.0.

'I like the hair.'

'Like? That's it?'

'You think it's age-appropriate?'

'What, are you kidding me?'

'Don't get me wrong. I think it's great. A new image. At your age.'

'Dig yourself in a little deeper.'

'Just takes getting used to. It helps hide the grey bits.'

A pair of fists in mock fighter mode. He backs away, laughing.

'Mae will love it. I say she'll go for the optimism.'

Still the smartass, just a more polished vocabulary.

He and Mae do hit it off, which is great, another definite plus in the divorce aftermath. When she entered the picture a few months ago, I braced myself for whatever. But, fingers crossed, it's all zip-a-dee-doo-dah so far.

Nick has been through the adventure of Samantha (my ex/ his mother) taking on a new partner, the tried-and-true police inspector, Frederick Olsen. Never thought I'd see the positive side of that scenario, but there it is, Nick's experience working in my favour.

'How about I go for a more youthful look? How about rolled-up trousers showing some funky sock?'

'At the risk of me disowning you.'

'That would save me a few bucks.'

There's no end in sight. What there is is the smell of roast chicken and vegetables, the bird having been dutifully marinated for twenty-four hours in buttermilk prior to entry in the oven.

The lad loves his roast chicken, and with the aromas emanating from the kitchen he opts for a truce. 'Tell you what,' he says. 'I'll set the table and we'll pretend you're no longer in your twenties.'

I let that go, because I, unlike some, know when to stop.

'How's IB going?' I ask a while later, after we've devoured a solid share of the main attraction and moved on to the rum cake and Häagen-Dazs.

'Fine. You know, a lot of work.'

A lot of work is good. Keeps him busy, out of trouble. Not that I've had anything much to complain about since he started high school. Every teenager has issues—some that parents know about, a lot they don't—but Nick seems to have worked things through, up to now at least. Never know what might pop up, but there it is. Deal with it when it happens.

He goes to Heart, as the students call it. Short for Holy Heart. Very short for Holy Heart of Mary High School. Big enough and diverse enough that like-minded students, whatever their interests or social skills, eventually find each other. Nick is thick with maybe a half-dozen of his peers—all fine with science and math, but big into the arts, without leaving sports behind. It's noticeably upped his comfort level from junior high. As we agree without saying it outright, it seems he's got his shit together.

Among Heart's academic choices is the International Baccalaureate program. Intense, heavy workload, no slack from beginning to end. A couple of his friends were applying, so Nick got it in his head that maybe he'd give it a shot. I wasn't so sure, his mother even less so. I knew he had the smarts. The question was whether he'd apply himself when the workload mushroomed. In the end, what do you do? We weren't about to discourage him from giving his brain a workout. We handed the young fellow our blessing, and he plunged in.

So far, so good.

Or as Nick says, 'So far, man, no shit hit no fan.'

It is less a reflection of how IB has expanded his verbal skills than his delight in sharing the wit of his friend Kofi.

Kofi is originally from Ghana and has been living in Canada since he was a young kid. His father teaches physics at the university. His mother has a catering business and the family also runs a spot at the weekend Farmer's Market, selling African food.

Nick and Kofi hit it off during their first year at Heart. Kofi shows up in the house with Nick sometimes, an all-around polite, easygoing kid, but obviously there's a side of Kofi I get to see only through Nick, including wily variations on over-used idioms.

Like 'When the going gets tough, then what the fuck, tough shit, keep going.'

What's to do but laugh. Nick used to try at least to temper his language around me. Not so much anymore. That particular gap has narrowed. Around his mother, likely not so much.

Nick and I have been through some of that tough shit together, stuff that levelled our take on the world. He helped save my bacon a couple of times—that's bound to change things up. As far as him swearing in front of me, I'd prefer the old Nick, but let's face it, who am I to mouth off about the odd curse word. That's him widening his boundaries. I like what I see. And so far, man (fingers crossed), no shit hit no fan.

Besides spending time with his father and roast chicken, Nick's here to pick up Gaffer. The little guy is spending the long weekend with him. Samantha was never keen to have the dog share her living space, but that, too, no longer results in any excrement hitting any fan. Largely due to the mediation efforts of Frederick, it appears. Yet another positive side of the man.

Gaffer, bag packed, is ready to go. He has no qualms about moving house, knowing it means having time with his other favourite person in the world, who has lots of energy for the romp-and-roll lifestyle that the dog has to do without when living with me.

'Say hi to Mae for me. Have fun in Fogo,' Nick says as he dons his jacket. I give him a hug.

'It'll be good to get away after all winter. We're looking forward to it.'

'I bet you are.' Nick grabs the bag that holds all the canine paraphernalia. I hand him Gaffer's leash, then bend down and rub the mutt's head. 'See ya, pal. Be good. No peeing in the periwinkle.' I hold open the door. 'I'll see you guys in a few days.'

From the outside step, Nick looks back. 'Enjoy yourself. I know you will.' He winks. 'Good luck.'

Yes, and goes down the steps, looks up at me with a puckish smile and winks again. As if he's out to embarrass a drinking buddy about a prospective frolic between the sheets. He's gone then, Gaffer tight at his heels.

Growing up a bit too quickly. That, or the father-son relationship needs further realignment. Something else to put on the back burner for future attention.

Fogo Island it is. For the May 24th/Victoria Day weekend. Pretty much a vestigial holiday, given that Queen Victoria is not much on anyone's mind these days. With all due respect, I'm sure, it's now known by some as the May two-four weekend. As in a two-four, two dozen beer.

Whatever, it marks the unofficial start of summer. That could mean anything from a bout of sloppy snow to the sun splitting the rocks. In Newfoundland you pay your money and you take your chances.

Fogo Island was Mae's idea. Got me excited from the get-go. The extra travel time is no big deal, given she's taking Friday off work. Four and a half hours to the ferry. Add a detour in Clarenville for an awesome breakfast at the Bare Mountain Coffee House, plus a generous wait time in the lineup to be sure of getting on the three-thirty run. Which means out of bed by six a.m., knocking back at least one cup of coffee before picking up Mae and heading off.

Yawning hour, but all systems will be up and running.

Let's step back for a moment. Some explanation is in order. Of how we have reached this point, when five months ago I had never laid eyes on the woman.

Mae owns a fabric store that caters to quilters. There are a slew in Newfoundland, even a few men, including Adam, relatively new partner of my long-time friend Jeremy. Adam's spare time, when it is not taken up with photography, is taken up with making quilts. Well, not quilts exactly, more wall hangings. All those separate pieces of fabric, perfectly joined. Amazing, when you think of it. To be honest, I haven't really thought of it, up until now.

Adam specializes in roosters. One-of-a-kind pieces that he sells on Etsy for hundreds of dollars. Roosters are big these days. Who knew? I tell Adam he's cock of the walk. Jeremy agrees.

So at Jeremy and Adam's Christmas dinner party, there is Mae sitting across from me. If this had been before Adam was on the scene, I would have known everyone, but with a new partner come new friends. All good.

All very good, in this case. We hit it off, Mae and I, from the opening exchange. Having indicated her fabric store connection to Adam, she clearly expected me to volunteer my own method of earning my keep.

'I call it dual occupancy. One half of me is a tour guide, the other half a private detective.' It usually leaves the recipient doubtful as to how to respond.

But in this case, not. 'Do the two ever meet?'

'As a matter of fact, they do.' I relate the incident in which someone on one of my tours was nudged to his death over a cliff below Signal Hill.

'I remember that. I followed the news stories at the time. It got quite complicated, if I recall correctly.'

'A lot to unravel.'

'That was you, unravelling?'

'It was my start.'

'How interesting. I always say if life is not interesting, you need to change jobs.'

The first vibe of kindred spirits. Candour that was bound to open doors.

In the course of the evening, our backstories emerge with satisfying ease.

Mae is roughly eight years younger. At this age, it's of no consequence (except, I chuckle, I qualified for the COVID vaccine before she did). She, too, has a child, by an early and only marriage, a merger she describes as 'a mismatch from day one.' It's well in the past. She's basically raised her daughter on her own, the father being in Ontario and out of the picture most of the time. Kayla is now twenty, working on a science degree.

There have been subsequent relationships, but, from what I gather, none she considered making permanent. Once hastily burned, twice shy.

Which, at this stage, works for both of us. She occasionally stays over, but we generally maintain a comfortable distance. Too early in the relationship to think about shared living space.

Which makes the four-day weekend an unacknowledged test, of sorts. We've not spent this much time together in a single stretch. No nerves, take it as it comes. We're out to enjoy ourselves. Eat, drink, hike, and be merry. On the go-go in Fogo.

The turnoff from the Trans-Canada is just as you enter Gander, the town where I lived and learned for the pre-university segment of my life, but with which I don't have much connection anymore. My sister still lives there, but there's no time to stop. Nor inclination, the sibling dynamics being what they are. Mae knows the situation and we breeze past the town limits without a word about it.

On the way to Farewell, where we'll pick up the ferry. Always good to arrive early, and here we are, well ahead of departure and sitting pretty in my red Toyota. Mae had the forethought to pack a couple of sandwiches, and not long after we've polished them off and stretched our legs, like clockwork, the MV *Veteran* comes into view.

It's sunny, albeit 12°C on land, which translates to time on deck bundled in winter coats. We're on open coastal waters, with icebergs adding to the refrigeration.

Yes, icebergs. Two of them, and well within sight. Shouldn't be surprised. We're in prime Iceberg Alley territory, where the glacial hulks drift down from Greenland and nestle along the coastline. And not far from the unrivalled town of Twillingate, Newfoundland's very own Iceberg Capital of the World.

Always an instinctive thrill to lay eyes on the sculpted mammoths. Mental note 1: Add Fogo Island to list of possible future tours. Mental note 2: Has there ever been a whisky made using iceberg water?

One of the bergs is pyramidal (and, might I add, not unlike the famed Pei pyramid covering the entrance to the Louvre). But slightly tilted, and with the sun glinting off a distinct blue vein of ice.

Mae is equally excited. 'A good luck omen,' she remarks. Needless to say, I'm all for getting lucky.

There's a brief ferry stop en route. Long enough for two vehicles to disembark and another three to come aboard. Change Islands is considerably smaller in size and head count than Fogo Island but very scenic, from what I've heard. A visit for another time. Right now we're geared up and ready for

Fogo, the largest of Newfoundland's offshore islands, a scenic, celebrated wonder in itself.

Odd name, Fogo. Unless you're Portuguese. In which case it means fire. So *Y del Fogo*. Isle of Fire. (Or in this case, isle of the fired up.)

The name befits a far-flung island in the North Atlantic that is near mythical in stature. Prehistoric occupation dating back five millennia. In 1598 penned on a French map as *I. de Fogo*, and again in 1632 as *Iles des Fogues*. One of the Four Corners of the World in the annals of the Flat Earth Society. Home to undaunted people who in the 1960s defied a government clamouring for them to resettle to the province's mainland. Its rockscape today shouldering an architecturally stunning resort hotel, Canada's best, the world's number three.

If that doesn't impress the wayfarer, the signs leading to its settlements surely will—Joe Batt's Arm, Tilting, Seldom-Come-By, Barr'd Islands. You'd have to be a hopeless crank to not feel the charm once you're off the ferry and heading north, toward Brimstone Head, that designated drop-off corner of the flat earth.

Mae has us booked into one of a pair of saltbox guesthouses within spitting distance of it. I'm not prone to walking in my sleep, so we're safe.

The view out the picture windows alone is worth the price, whatever it is. Full ocean view—rock-strewn beach, waves lapping ashore, occasionally smacking over rocks. Gulls and iceberg bits.

Mae insisted the trip be her treat and I didn't ask questions. Nor feel any guilt, since it's likely well beyond my budget. While I'm still in recovery mode after COVID wreaked havoc with the tour business, lockdown seems to have left a lot of people at home with loads of time to sew. Mae added an online component and her shop thrived. Her customers sew, and I reap.

The deal is when we're not eating out, I'm house chef. Tonight that means cod from the Fogo Island Co-op. Not netted and dumped ashore, but handlined in the centuries-old way, bled, washed, and iced at sea. The boneless fillet that stretches across the cutting board is the freshest and finest to be procured anywhere. You'll find it in some of best restaurants in Toronto and Calgary, and on the plates of a couple of townies out for the weekend, seated next to each other before the postcard seascape, glasses of buttery Chardonnay in hand.

The cod I've seared in oil and butter. Seasoned with Newfoundland sea salt and pepper, one quick turn in the pan, and as soon as it flakes apart, that's it, on to the dinner plate. With a side of dandelion greens picked in a field not far from the house, sautéed with garlic and the salt.

God, does it get any better? Do the taste buds not thrive, foreshadowing what lies ahead for the rest of the evening and into the night?

I'm not good at hiding the early stages of lust. Gently caressing Mae's hand as it rests on the table would be your first clue.

She looks at me and smiles. 'I wonder if dandelion is an aphrodisiac?'

'I'm thinking yes.'

'Hold that thought. It's a long evening.' She pecks me on the cheek.

She gathers up the plates and carries them to the kitchen. Obviously practised in keeping the man at bay until such time as her mood parallels his own.

'Have you not noticed the size of the clawfoot tub?' she says, sliding the plates into a sink of sudsy water.

Gulp that Chardonnay and follow with a manly groan.

'You're so subtle, Sebastian.'

Mae, as she revealed over dinner, has preliminary plans for

the evening. She's (quote, unquote) 'all excited' about checking out a quilt shop in Tilting.

'My soul is fed with needle and thread,' she says with a chuckle. I respond with another groan, one not quite so manly.

The shop is a half-hour away. In time a certain eagerness on my part does surface, given there's a lot other than a quilt shop to anticipate in venturing to Tilting. Twenty years ago, every inch of the town was designated a Registered Heritage District and a national historic site. Imagine—you wake up in the morning, go to the bathroom, get dressed, step outside with a cup of coffee and a muffin, and you're in the depths of your country's history. Day in, day out. It's like living on a documentary film set.

Tilting has a special Irish lilt. Not only the name, the origin of which is said to be unknown. (I'm thinking something to do with the gait of the first Irish fisherman to settle here after a night on the whisky.) Regardless, there's a three-hundred-year-old lilt in the language and customs, in the wealth of fishing sheds and stages set into the shoreline. In the vegetable plots and time-worn root cellars. All capable of leaving photographers weak at the knees.

Even the shop is in on the lilting. It's called (what else?) Quilting in Tilting.

We turn into the parking spot. 'I'll try to keep it short,' Mae says, 'but you know quilters when they get together . . .'

'I know . . . time is immaterial.' The cravings might be on hold, but I'm still up for a spirited quip.

'It's like you and whisky, Sebastian. Time means nothing when there's another stiff one to be had.'

Yes, I've met my match. And yes, hand in hand, still smiling, we take to the path leading to three steps and the front door. In its window a sign reads: 'Quilting is our fate! / Open 10–8.'

I check my phone. 8:12. 'You know quilters,' says Mae; 'they always lose track of time.'

I try the door, and sure enough it's unlocked. Mae walks in and I follow dutifully. It's not large, but it is colourfully impressive. Walls covered with quilts and hangings of numerous sizes and patterns. More quilts stacked on tables and spread over display racks. Shelves brimming with bolts of fabric, baskets with small, folded samples of them. More tables with tools of the quilting trade, including a baffling array of unrecognizable gadgets.

We've arrived at a prime time. It being the start of the tourist season, the shop is fully stocked. The owner has been quilting up a storm all winter, and the results have not yet been scoured by the quilt-coveting lot sure to show up by mid-summer.

Gertie is the owner's name, but there's no Gertie to be seen. She's in a back room, no doubt, and will emerge in due course. In the meantime there's valuable quilting chat time wasting away. Mae is feeling the deprivation. She has me to fill the gap, but apparently it's just not the same.

'So beautifully done,' she says, standing in front of a bed-size quilt that covers much of one wall. 'She has great colour sense. And her corners match perfectly.'

'Always a good sign.'

'And don't you love the pattern? It's called Double Irish Chain.'

'Irish I understand. Why double and not single or triple?'

'You're hopeless,' says Mae. 'At least when it comes to quilts.'

I appreciate the qualifier. 'I'm eager to learn anything you can teach me.'

'We'll start you off with strip piecing and see how you do.'

'I'm up for that.'

She smiles, shakes her head, poking me in the ribs as she moves on.

Gertie still hasn't made an appearance. Which goes to show how trusting people are on this island. Some meandering scoundrel could have walked away with several armloads of quilts by now. Then again, 'thief' doesn't fit the profile of anyone who frequents quilt shops.

'Hello. Is there someone around?' Mae calls out finally. Of course, there has to be. Perhaps in the washroom.

No answer. We wait a while longer. Suddenly I'm thinking the worst. Maybe the woman had a heart attack.

'I'll take a peek,' says Mae, walking in the direction of the quilted curtain that hangs in front of the entrance to what must be a back room. She pauses. 'Think I should?'

'Go for it.' My first aid training at the ready.

Mae draws back the curtain, tentatively, just enough to peer inside.

Her hand covers her mouth. The curtain falls back in place. She turns to me, her stiffened upper body falling against the door frame.

'Oh my Jesus!'

I hold her tight to me with one arm. I raise the other and draw back the curtain.

Oh my Jesus is right.

First aid will be useless. I know it immediately, before I separate myself from Mae, before I bend down and pull back the blood-soaked quilt partially covering the woman in order to check her pulse.

She's bled to death. There's a spent river of blood, far too broad for that not to be the cause. The source is a gash to her neck. From below her right ear protrude the closed handles of a pair of scissors. They are small, sized for delicate fingers. At first glance too small to inflict such trauma.

The point of entry proved critical. Her carotid artery has been punctured.

There was a time when my reaction might have paralleled Mae's. The sight of a dead body, even as hideous as this, no longer upends me. 'Call the police,' I tell her. 'Then lock the front door until they arrive.'

While Mae walks back into the store, I take a deep breath and retrieve my phone from my pocket. Without moving from where I stand, I record the scene in a dozen pictures, including close-ups of the wound, the quilt, and the table that bears the victim's sewing machine.

Turning away in relief, I join Mae in the store. She wraps her arms around me and sinks her head into my shoulder. She's shaking uncontrollably.

I hold her tighter. The shaking lessens but is not about to disappear. 'The RCMP will be here soon,' I tell her. 'They'll take care of it.'

A failed attempt to calm her. There will be no taking care of it. Obviously it's murder, obviously the hideousness of it is not about to be contained.

'I can't get the picture of the stork scissors out of my mind,' she stutters. 'How absolutely awful.'

'*Stork* scissors?'

Mae leads me to the table where quilting implements are displayed. She lifts the packaging to give me a closer view. Small, delicate scissors in the shape of a stork, its beak a pair of pointed blades, its elongated body ending in feet that rest atop the finger holes. Beautifully fashioned. Gold- and nickel-plated, it would seem.

'Hardly an instrument of murder. But in the right hands . . .'

I must be careful. There's the danger—that comes from experience—of appearing callous and detached, carelessly professional, while Mae struggles to hold herself together.

I hear the RCMP vehicle pull up outside, sooner than expected. Thankfully no flashing lights, no siren. I hold open the door for the officer who has emerged from the car and is just coming up the steps.

She moves smartly inside, pleased to have arrived so quickly. 'Corporal Juillard. I was in Joe Batt's when the call came in.'

Joe Batt's Arm, a few minutes away. She's taken us for locals.

'What seems to be the problem?'

'Murder,' Mae blurts out, still in tears. 'Gertie has been murdered.'

It's so much more than the corporal would ever have expected. Nobody is ever murdered on Fogo Island.

'Are you certain?' she asks, her skepticism showing.

I lead her to the back room, to the all-too-vivid scene of the crime.

Her first look is probably implanting itself in her mind for a lifetime.

She comes to an abrupt stop. She stiffens. 'My God.'

The corporal looks to be in her mid-twenties. There's a chance there'll be another murder scene in her future, when she moves on to other detachments. But certainly none more bloody.

'My God,' she repeats.

It's as effusive as the RCMP are likely to get. 'Are you okay?'

No police officer is about to admit to anything less. She edges closer to the body.

I assure her there's nothing to be done for the woman. 'I checked her pulse. She's certainly dead.'

Corporal Juillard is on her phone immediately. To call in more officers, more senior ones. I recall seeing the Fogo Island detachment at the junction of the main road and the road to Joe Batt's Arm and Tilting. The backup will take at least a quarter of an hour.

Corporal Juillard steels herself and surveys the room closely, being careful not to compromise the crime scene.

Distraction might alleviate her queasiness. 'Did you know her?' I ask. Not an unreasonable question, given the whole island has only a couple of thousand inhabitants. And as a business owner, Gertie would have had a higher profile than most.

'The store has the best selection of thread on the island,' she responds limply. 'I don't quilt, but I sew.'

I see. Quilting in Tilting—the go-to shop for sewers of all persuasions. A loyal clientele it seems.

'If you're a sewist, you knew Gertie.'

Sewist? New one on me. I guess 'sewer' has all those other, negative connotations.

We join Mae, who has returned to the display of stork scissors. She's staring at them, still in disbelief.

'The murder weapon,' I inform the corporal.

'I thought I recognized the handles.'

A sewist would of course. Unlike Mae, she's not taken aback that the scissors could actually kill someone.

'There was a case where a man was murdered with a dessert spoon.' A bit of trivia I picked up in my PI training. A move to help ease the tension.

'Are you serious?' says Mae.

I wouldn't be anything but serious, given the situation. 'Back of the head. Ruptured artery. Bleeding to the brain. All documented.'

The reference goes nowhere. But then the backup comes in the door. Just in time.

A fresh pair of officers. The detachment must be pretty well empty.

They make no effort to introduce themselves. The urgency of Corporal Juillard's phone call leads them straight to the dead body.

'My God,' says one.

'*Sacrament!*' exclaims the other, blowing my theory of police uneffusiveness.

They turn out to be Staff Sergeant Lambert and Corporal Leblanc. Despite the staggering wallop to their routine, they take care to retain their efficiency. The staff sergeant checks for the non-existent pulse, then is on her phone to call in a doctor for official confirmation. There is the need to establish a police perimeter and contain the crime scene. And arrangements for photographic documentation of the same. She steps outside with her phone for what I assume is private consultation with her superiors at divisional headquarters. No doubt more officers will be on the way.

Only after that does Staff Sergeant Lambert require our undivided attention. She has questions and expects an extensive statement from each of us. I'm impressed with her confident attention to detail. I suspect her previous posting was an urban, crime-riddled one. She may well have headed east as a way of recovering from the stress of the frightful street crime one hears about in Calgary or Vancouver, only to have idyllic Fogo Island let her down. That would be my theory.

When she finally closes her notebook she asks, 'Are you a south coast Synard?'

I wouldn't expect it of a mainlander.

'I grew up in Gander.'

'Gander was my first posting. Synard is not a surname I recall. Fairly common on the south coast. I'm from Marystown.'

I see. But in between Gander and Fogo came urban mainland Canada, no doubt. I don't ask. There are greater priorities. 'There will be an autopsy, of course?'

'The body will be airlifted to St. John's. Once the probe of the crime scene is complete.'

Confirmation that there'll be a small squad of uniforms

aboard the first ferry in the morning.

'You are both remaining on the island for the next few days, I assume?' she says.

Her subtle way of noting we haven't been eliminated as suspects in the murder.

We're free to go, however, with the agreement that we check in at the detachment in the morning. And that we not relate any of what has taken place to the general public.

Corporal Juillard has been working on how to proceed with notifying the dead woman's next of kin. 'As I recall from conversations I had with her, she lived alone.'

It's no surprise she's aware of this. Sewists would be talkers.

I check my phone. It's been more than an hour and a half since Mae and I arrived. The scene, as gruesome as it is, has been normalized by the passage of time. The curtain closed, the chatter between us has turned near congenial. Odd, that: it's like corridor talk at a funeral home. Gertie wasn't a friend; she has quickly become a corpse and raw evidence in a criminal investigation.

It is only when I open the door for us to head to the Toyota that the full impact strikes me. Beyond the yellow tape barrier that Corporal Leblanc has set in place stand a half-dozen citizens of Tilting, all needing to know just what is going on. Two police cars are alarming. They fear the worst. They are not dressed for the long wait, with the temperature having dropped once the sun went down.

'Buddy, what's up?'

He's the youngest and boldest of the lot. His hands are deep in the pockets of his jacket, black with neon green stripes, emblazed with the word Yamaha.

'You'll hear from the RCMP. I'm afraid I can't comment.'

'Not good, is it, buddy?'

'As I said, it's in the hands of the police.'

'She's me great-aunt. Is she hurt?'

That unleashes a chorus of connections. Cousin. Church choir member. Quilter. Noticeably, no children or siblings.

We press ahead to our vehicle. 'Sorry I can't answer your questions.'

'You're not from around here,' says the young fellow as we get in the car.

We wouldn't be holding back if we were. We'd at least be preparing them for the worst. I've suddenly become a pretentious mainlander.

But it will have to be tomorrow before they find out that is far from the case. And tomorrow is when my overpowering urge to investigate what happened to the unfortunate woman will truly take hold.

LOVER'S KNOT

THERE'S JUST THE two of us talking it over on the couch, the sea before us, faintly lit by a partial moon. We had brought out a red to uncork but decided that more Chardonnay would be less of a reminder of the scene we just left.

'What happens now?' Mae asks.

There's a quick answer from someone who knows very well what will happen. 'The RCMP will undertake a deep probe of the crime scene. Question family members and branch out from there. Establish a presence at the ferry terminal. Record who's leaving the island, do background checks on anyone who looks suspicious. The same goes for any flights. In the meantime, the body gets sent to St. John's for a forensic autopsy.'

'And you, Sebastian, where do you see yourself fitting in?'

I do, of course, see myself 'fitting in.' 'This is no ordinary murder, Mae. Here is an everyday, conventional, homespun woman (or so it would appear at this point at least), who you'd never imagine could be the target of such a monstrous act. Here is a good-willed, peaceable outport community thrown into turmoil by someone you'd never expect to exist here—a nefarious sociopath. The immediate question becomes: Is the murderer from outside, or is that someone a permanent resident of Fogo Island? If it's the former, then, with background checks, potential suspects should be relatively easy to identify. And if the latter, then we have fewer than two thousand adult inhabitants to choose from. Eliminate the slow-moving and easily disoriented and that number drops even further.'

'So you think it is only a matter of time before the RCMP make an arrest?'

'One would hope. This is where I come in.' I hold up my phone. 'I made a record of the scene before the police arrived. That puts me on a rather strong footing. As for an autopsy, that's bound to be of little consequence. It's obvious how the woman died. The key is moving swiftly, crossing paths with potential suspects, and picking up on any clues the cops might overlook. Are you with me?'

She hesitates. I know what she's thinking. I'm about to bugger up the plans she put in place for the weekend. There goes the romantic getaway, out the picture window.

Not necessarily. I'm sure we can fit some things in. The most urgent, the most burning, the ones toward which, despite everything, we still feel an inclination.

'Do you mean "with you" in the sense that I understand where you're coming from? Or "with you" as in teaming up with you. Your partner, so to speak?'

To be honest, I hadn't considered the second option. I hadn't really thought she'd be keen, or even interested, given her reaction when she discovered the body. I figured that encounter alone was more than enough for her to deal with. But I'm not about to underestimate the woman and have it gnaw at our relationship. Been through that one before.

'I owe it to Gertie,' she says, before I formulate an answer. 'Quilters are soulmates, bonded by the love of what we do. Crime inflicted on one is crime inflicted on us all. And to think it took place right in her shop, with a pair of her own scissors. There can be only one answer.'

'Might I offer a piece of advice?'

She takes an extended sip of the Chardonnay.

'Tread easy. Where there's one murder, another might not be far behind. Keep your wits about you. Whoever murdered Gertie was not in a frame of mind that understands reason. It has all the makings of a crime of passion.'

'I'm game.'

I'm not sure whether to breathe a sigh of relief or one of trepidation. A girl Friday? I have a feeling the term is offensive these days, even in jest. Best to steer clear. No, Mae will undoubtedly be an asset. The fact that she's a quilter, that alone could give us a significant edge.

I angle my phone away from her and flick through the pictures, stopping at a close-up of the quilt that covered the victim. I edit the image to eliminate the upper border soaked with blood.

'Have a look. What can you tell me about this?'

I'm not sure she recognizes it as the quilt covering Gertie. She may have been too traumatized at the time for it to have registered.

She holds the phone closer. 'Lover's Knot,' she says.

I'm not getting it.

'The quilt pattern. Lover's Knot.'

Really? Mae has taken all of two minutes to make herself invaluable to the investigation. 'It must be the quilt Gertie was working on when she was killed. It's the one the killer threw over her dead body. In which case, are you thinking what I'm thinking?'

'Lover's Knot,' she says. 'Crime of passion.'

'Exactly.' I put down the phone and take Mae's hand in mine. I'm feeling the thrill of partnership. 'We're a match.'

Under normal circumstances she might roll her eyes. Instead she chuckles quietly as I lean across to the lamp on the end table and turn it out, the last light source in the room. This calls for nature's moonglow, the perfect accompaniment to my easing us to a prone position along the length of the couch.

My lips sink tenderly but passionately into hers. If there is an anticipatory moan it's my hormones confirming that they've been hanging back in idleness for too long.

My hand wanders under her sweater, eager for that silken touch.

'Really, Sebastian?'

Abortive moaning. It takes a moment for my attention to realign.

'Is something the matter?'

'We have just been thrown into the midst of a gruesome murder. How can you have anything else on your mind?'

I don't have an answer for that. The fact is I can compartmentalize. A fact that would be unwise to share. 'I'm not really sure.'

'Don't you feel it would be disrespectful?'

Quilter to quilter maybe. 'I can see that, but you know . . .' No point in going there.

'I think we better call it a night. I'll take a hot shower. That might help me sleep.'

Yes, there you go. Nothing like murder to speed up the end to the evening. Quell the libido. 'Sure thing.'

I sit up, dutifully pour another glass of wine, and wait my turn for the shower. A cold one would seem in order.

HITHER AND YON

FIRST THINGS FIRST. A substantial breakfast, given that we don't know where the day will take us and just when we'll find time for lunch. Mae is up and dressed and scrambling eggs before I discharge myself from the bed. I regard her eagerness, in contrast to the lack of it the evening before, puts me in a bit of a funk.

Her smile widens as she sets the table. A small glass of freshly squeezed orange juice stands beside each plate and its display of eggs, back bacon, whole grain toast, and avocado slices drizzled with what may well be a balsamic vinegar reduction.

'Very nice,' I admit.

'C'mon, Sebastian, snap out of it. Mood is everything. Coffee?'

Yes, indeed, notably eager to set all else aside and start the day fresh and focused. As for me, I refuse to wallow in wasted opportunities.

The coffee does what coffee is meant to do. I can't be anything but alert to the challenge of tracking down who is responsible for the nasty business in Tilting. I'm nothing if not up for it.

By nine fifteen we're in the parking lot of the RCMP detachment, primed to learn what, if anything, has transpired overnight. Prior to making an entrance, however, we need to strategize. I see no reason to tell the troops that I sometimes work as a private investigator. It would complicate matters, get them thinking I might somehow impede their own investigation.

'What they don't know won't hurt them.'

'Agreed,' says Mae. 'Although there may come a point . . .'

'When they figure it out for themselves. Agreed. We'll cross that bridge when we come to it.'

We exit the vehicle and head for their home turf, ready to traverse that average Joe/police officer divide.

Staff Sergeant Lambert exits her office to greet us in the reception area, the chevrons denoting her rank looking neat and crisp on the shoulders of her casual, everyday work uniform.

'Good morning. I hope you both slept well. I know it couldn't have been easy. We're still pretty shaken ourselves.'

This is a good start. When the police admit to being rattled, you know there's common ground to be had.

'It was dreadful, absolutely.' I stop at that. Restraint is important in any exchange with the police. You never want them thinking you don't have your emotions under control.

'We were devastated,' Mae announces. 'The poor woman, what a tragedy! We're both still reeling from it.'

Apparently we needed to strategize a little longer.

The staff sergeant smiles knowingly. 'Come into my office, if you would. I have a few things that need clarification.'

No surprise there, of course. Before the squad sent by divisional headquarters shows up, the local detachment will need to have all its ducks in order.

We're joined by Corporal Juillard, who has just arrived for work. She's not looking particularly sharp. We discover from her conversation with the staff sergeant that after completing the unenviable task of informing the next of kin, she returned to the crime scene and was left to guard it alone for several hours. It's no wonder the corporal is looking the worse for wear.

There's little time for sympathy from the staff sergeant, however. It's straight on to the matter at hand. That would be us, the co-discoverers of the body. 'Would you mind telling me why you went to Quilting in Tilting when you did, after hours? Why not wait until the next day, when you would have had more time?'

In a pleasant enough tone, but you know she's probing, working all the angles. I take my time. 'A good question.'

Mae, on the other hand, steps directly up to the plate. 'We had hoped to get there before closing time. We decided to take the chance. If you're into fabric and quilting, you get the urge, you know.'

The officer doesn't know. She no doubt has things that take up her spare time, but sewing is not one of them. I'm thinking maybe fishing and hunting. Exercise equipment.

Corporal Juillard, fortunately, does know the urge. This is where her sewist background plays to our benefit. 'I would have to agree,' she inserts. 'Fabric shops are addictive.'

The staff sergeant might be willing to accept what must be to her mind a curious obsession, but she needs a strong comeback to retain control. She looks straight at me.

'It was convenient then, Mr. Synard, that a private investigator showed up directly following the murder?'

I draw in more air, to replace what had just been unceremoniously expelled. 'I would have to say . . . in all honesty . . . yes.'

'I see.'

I have the distinct feeling she's not buying into it, not completely. As for me, there's a bigger question. How did she find out my line of work so quickly? Up late scouring the internet? Newspaper stories about past cases?

'I've been on the phone to headquarters in St. John's this morning. Inspector Bowmore passes along her regards.'

I see. I fake amusement. Ah, Inspector Bowmore, who was at the centre of the last murder case I was involved in. Shall we say our rapport at the time was memorable.

Should I be surprised? No. Should I have realized the RCMP's provincial crime unit would be clued in from the start? Yes. And that Inspector Bowmore would have a lot to offer the rural staff sergeant who would be seeking direction as she proceeds with the investigation.

My look of amusement wears thin. 'The next time you're speaking with her, please pass along my regards.'

'She was complimentary about your work in the past.'

Really? I have to say I didn't expect it. 'That's very good of her.'

I leave it at that. Inspector Bowmore and I have had our differences of opinion. Still, it was good of her to put me in a positive light. Especially now that the staff sergeant suspects I'll be heading down the investigative path myself.

No point in having her probe to confirm that. 'It's my intention to move ahead with an investigation of my own.'

'I see.'

'Let's be clear—any leads I pick up, anything that might be of use to you, I'll pass along.'

I just don't commit to how long that might take. Say I've uncovered some tantalizing bit of info and I know that by calling in the cops I might just jeopardize uncovering more . . . well, of course, I won't be jumping the gun.

I doubt she's ever had dealings with a PI. For sure not during her time on Fogo Island. I'm an alien species.

'No need to worry, I won't be in the way.'

A certain amount of skepticism is to be expected. Hard for me to tell just how deep it's running.

'Who's hired you, Mr. Synard? I realize private investigators have to make a living.'

The staff sergeant thinks she just tripped me up. 'In this case . . .'

'I have. I hired him,' Mae announces.

The skepticism just deepened. She turns to Mae. 'Really. I'm surprised. I didn't think you had a personal relationship with the deceased.'

'Personal in the sense we were in the same line of business. In the sense we both loved quilts and quilting.' Mae stops at that.

Which only accentuates the fact that it's calculated bullshit.

Her answer is definitely not doing it for the staff sergeant. As Mae is well aware. She digs deeper. 'You may have heard it said that quilters are kindred spirits. That we're bonded by the love of what we do. You could say that crime inflicted on one is crime inflicted on us all.'

Yes, you might say that, a second time. It worked once, why not give it another shot?

Staff Sergeant Lambert struggles to work up a response. Frustration brews.

'I can see that.' It's Corporal Juillard, oblivious to the danger of interfering with her boss's line of questioning. Kicking in again with her own response, for what it's worth.

Complicating it for the staff sergeant. Two against one.

'Laypersons such as ourselves,' I add, 'don't appreciate quilting, or quilters. I've discovered they speak a different language. They communicate on a level we don't truly understand. They're a breed apart.'

There we are. Make that three against one.

'I see,' the staff sergeant says eventually. More to put an end to it than anything, I suspect.

Nevertheless, Mae rushes in to solidify her perspective. 'I'm not paying him much, of course. The minimum. The bare minimum.' Make that A+ for additional effort and for making it very slightly more palatable to the staff sergeant.

The policewoman says no more. And so we move on.

And what an appropriate time for a flurry of activity at the front entrance of the detachment. It appears reinforcements have arrived.

'Staff Sergeant Lambert, we're here. Ready to sink our teeth into it.'

The officer is not aware, of course, that the average Joe is in the building. When I emerge from the office ahead of the other three, he puts a quick damper on it.

There are three men of a wide age range, from freshly schooled to likely nearing retirement, to judge by the well-expanded midsection. Still within the weight requirements, one assumes, though definitely at the limit. He is the one whose voice was on high alert.

Their eagerness to get to the action is not so easily quelled. It remains in their ambitious smiles and keen, well-lit eyes. I have the feeling that, had Mae and I not made an appearance, they would be rubbing their hands together. Much too long behind desks would be my opinion.

Their lips tighten as they make a path for us to exit, suddenly focused on not letting the minutest hint of their game plan escape. Not that I have any interest in knowing what it is.

It's a tight squeeze past them and their cases, holding what I take to be high-tech forensic equipment. They're anxious to put it to use. To gear up and go at it before the crime scene ages any further.

'Good day, gentlemen. And good luck.'

They'll need it. Hopefully they're smart enough to know that technology only gets you so far in criminal investigation. In contrast to my approach, which is person-to-person, one-on-one contact. Let's get out into the community and talk to people. Let's see what nuggets of information lead to other nuggets. Let's see the pieces of the jigsaw start to accumulate and, over time, fall into place.

'So,' says Mae, having just gotten a taste of the intrigue taking shape within the official ranks and appearing more eager than ever to take the plunge. 'Where do we start?'

That edge of excitement suggests she's not just along for the ride, or even to sit cool and collected in the passenger seat.

A measured caution, a word to the wise. 'A gentle reminder that the less attention we draw to ourselves, the more headway we're likely to make.'

'Noted,' she says. No offence taken. So far, so good.

'We'll find out where Gertie lived and see what that brings to the plate.'

Simple enough, and in a community the size of Tilting the obvious source of information is the general store, in this case Hurley's, on the main road through town. To quote one Google reviewer, 'Everything you may need from spaghetti to spark plugs.'

I love these places. I'm a stranger prepared to be charmed after my opening line. 'Good morning. And how are you today?'

The cashier is a young woman in a snug tank top, no more than twenty, I would guess.

'Gutted,' she says.

It's far from a normal day in Tilting.

'We heard what happened. It must be terribly hard on everyone.'

'Gutted and heartbroken, the whole lot of us.'

'Especially her family.'

'She treated everyone like family.'

She gives no ground. I'm about to take another stab at

striking the right note when Mae steps in. 'We're both very sorry,' she says. 'To lose a wife and mother is one thing. But in this way—how awful. I can't imagine.'

'Gertie was never married. She never had children. But still, Jason don't know what hit him. Gertie was like a mother to him.' Jason Pottle, she tells us, Gertie's great-nephew.

Well done, Mae. But I'm all for giving it another go myself.

'She lived alone then?'

'What choice did she have?'

'Of course.'

'She had her shop,' says Mae. 'That would have kept her busy. Anyone who loved quilts and came to Fogo Island knew right where to go.'

'Oh my God, yes. Her shop meant the world to her. And to think . . .' The young woman wipes away a tear.

'She lived not far from her shop, I take it?' I'm certain my question doesn't sound presumptuous.

She fails to respond. Until Mae adds, 'The poor woman kept her health then. Quilting can be hard on your body. All that sitting and bending over the sewing machine.'

'Yes, my dear, more fit than I'll ever be. She walked everywhere. She didn't have a car and it was a bit of a hike to her shop. But of course Jace helped her out if the weather was bad.'

'Of course.' Me again. Jace, short for Jason, I take it.

I think that's as far as we're likely to get. I begin to look around the store. We should buy something, a show of gratitude. It'll help keep us on friendly terms. I pick an ice cream bar from the freezer. My go-to choice in these situations.

'Mae,' I call over, holding it up for her to see. 'Can I get you one as well?' Mae is just finishing up what appears to have been a friendly conversation. She joins me by the freezer.

'Don't be chintzy,' she whispers.

By the time we reassemble at the counter Mae has a loaf of

bread and several bottles of homemade jams and jellies, pickles and relishes.

The young woman is very pleased. 'Mother made them last fall and kept them in the cellar over the winter. All her own recipes. She's a great one for preserving. And the bread she baked yesterday.'

The ice cream bar looks a bit limp. I quickly retrieve a credit card from my wallet. 'All on the one bill.' It seems to redeem me slightly in her eyes. Maybe she appreciates a man who's eager to pay.

Mae gathers up the loot, minus the bar, and inserts it all into the tote bag she had the forethought to bring along. 'Thanks very much, Teagan. We'll be in again, I'm sure.'

'Remember—first right past the church, white two-storey. You can't miss it.'

I'm well into the ice cream bar by the time we're through the door. It's very good, one of the more expensive choices in the freezer.

'The Catholic church, I assume?' A redundant question. Just trying to keep the conversation flowing.

'There's only one.'

Fair enough. It goes without saying that Tilting was settled by solid Irish Catholics.

Within minutes we're parked on the shoulder of the road in front of the white two-storey. So easy when you know what you're looking for.

There's a blue pickup in the driveway. It's seen better days.

I wouldn't have been surprised to see a cop car. It has to be a site of interest, but it would seem all RCMP eyes are fixed on the scene of the crime, for the moment at least.

There's a path to a wide veranda and the front door. It opens before we reach it. We were seen heading up the driveway.

It's the young fellow from the night before, the one who

spoke to me outside the quilt shop, the great-nephew in the Yamaha jacket. Jason or Jace, we now know.

He recognizes us. It seems to alter what he was about to say. 'I'm here to keep an eye on the place. Cops asked me to.'

'We're sorry about your great-aunt. We hope you understand why we couldn't say anything last evening.'

His face stiffens. Fight it as he might, he can't hold back the emotion.

'You shouldn't be here by yourself,' Mae says, the voice of a mother. 'This is too much for you to deal with. Let's have a cup of coffee together.'

He's unsure. He's been entrusted with stopping anyone from coming inside. The forensic guys have yet to arrive.

'We're the ones who discovered her.'

It puts us in a different category. 'You knew her then?' he says, with a shade more interest.

'I knew about her store,' Mae says. 'We'd stopped by to have a look.'

'The cops won't say much. Was it awful?'

'We can't lie.' It's the best I can offer the young man.

He wants to know more. He wants to invite us in, but he won't.

'I'll tell you what,' says Mae. 'You fellows stay here. I'll run up to the Tilting Cup and bring us back some coffee.'

Before Jason has too long to think about it, she's off to the coffee shop we noticed driving through town.

Jason remembers some folding lawn chairs in the shed near the house. He retrieves three and sets them out on the veranda.

I like the opportunity to be alone with him. 'You need to know, Jason. It *was* awful. There was blood everywhere. Your aunt was murdered and at this point the cops have no clue who did it.' I could stop there and give him the chance to react, but no, there's more I throw at him. 'Just between you and me,

I happen to be a private investigator and I'm as hell-bent as the cops are to find out who did it. Are you game to help?'

It's a lot I know. But I'm looking for an automatic response. He loved Gertie. He's seething. Twenty-year-olds want revenge. That's their priority.

'Game to kill the fucking bastard.'

That's it. That's what I'm after. Though I can't go that far. 'Put the bastard behind bars.'

'No, fucking kill him.'

By the time Mae returns, her hands full, Jason has settled down somewhat. He heads back to the shed and returns with a small table.

Mae sets down the coffee, sugar, and cream, and a cardboard tray of brownies.

'Your aunt was very special to you,' Mae says, once Jason has had his first mouthful of brownie.

He hesitates, though not for long. 'She helped me a lot after Mom passed away. She helped me get through school. If it wasn't for her, I wouldn't have my electrical.'

He means his training as an electrician. He tells us he's got a job as an apprentice at the Fogo Island Inn, work that will lead to his journeyman certification.

'We're sorry about your mom.'

'Thank you,' he says, without wanting to go further.

'Had you noticed anything strange about Gertie in recent days? Anything at all.'

'That's what I don't understand. I had supper at her house two nights ago. If anything, she was even more cheerful than she usually is. It's not like she was in any trouble. Or anxious about anything.'

'It came out of the blue, then,' I say. 'Which makes me think that whoever did it was a stranger to her.'

'What was he after?' Jason puzzles over the big question—

motivation. 'Did the cops check the cash register? Wouldn't have been much money in it.'

'I did. A few tens and twenties, a couple of fives and some coin. Not much and still there.'

Mae looks at me, surprised she hadn't seen me do it, or she hadn't been told. You go about these things surreptitiously when you're on a case and the cops aren't around. You keep it to yourself, store it away in case you have use for it. Like now.

'The cash would have been the take for the day,' Mae says, exhibiting her knowledge of such matters, implying it would have been smarter of me to have told her. 'Unless it's something small, people pay with credit cards. For quilts they certainly would.'

'Anything stolen, do you think?'

'Hard to know.'

Not for Mae. 'No one murders a woman to steal her quilts. That makes no sense. Unless . . .'

'Unless what?'

'Unless whoever did it has no sense to begin with.'

'Exactly what I've been thinking,' says Jason. 'Whoever did this was not in his right fucking mind.'

Succinct and focused. Jason is getting more and more hepped up about the case, translating, I hope, to his full participation.

'We'll keep in touch. If you're good with that.'

He nods. I tell him where we're staying and we exchange cell numbers.

I feel positive. I feel we're on a good track. Only one thing.

'Best if we keep this to ourselves.'

'No worry there. I'm good at keeping my mouth shut about stuff. Ask me girlfriends.'

He isn't being funny. But perhaps more like himself. I feel some of the weight has lifted.

It'll take time. A long time in his case, considering how large a role Gertie played in his life. We're about to clear away the coffee things and head off when a truck pulls into the driveway.

Jason stands up and walks toward it. An older man emerges. They embrace, awkwardly, and for longer than men normally would. His father perhaps?

They talk, not something I can hear, but I sense what they're saying. They walk together in our direction as we step off the veranda.

'This is Kaleb. He's been doing some carpentry work for my aunt. He only found out this morning, coming across on the ferry.'

Kaleb is distraught.

'It was an unbelievable shock to everyone,' I say to him.

He shakes his head in disbelief. He can't speak.

'Kaleb lives on Change Islands. He's been replacing her kitchen cabinets.'

'I saw her yesterday morning,' he manages.

Jason finishes it for him. 'Before she went off to the shop for the day.'

'And she appeared to be fine?' Mae asks.

He takes a deep breath. 'Yes. Ask Connie.'

Connie, we learn, is Kaleb's wife. Yesterday she came over to Fogo with him for the day, to shop and visit friends. The three of them had tea together before they went about their day.

This explanation prompts Kaleb to step away and call his wife. When he returns, he's more upset than ever. 'Connie is beside herself. She can't believe it.'

In the meantime, Kaleb is not allowed in the house. He's doubly confused because he has no idea when he might be able to finish his work, or if he ever will.

'The cops will want to talk to you,' Jason says.

There's that, too. He's now a 'person of interest,' as the cops would term him. He might or might not have something to add to their investigation.

'They know where to find me.'

He turns and walks away. He climbs aboard his truck and drives off. Back to the ferry terminal, we assume, to catch the boat on its next trip, back to Change Islands.

The impact of the murder has spread throughout the island and beyond. When we drive by Quilting in Tilting, there's a trail of cars along the shoulder of the road and a large group of the idle and curious assembled outside the yellow tape.

There's no point in stopping on the off chance it might lead somewhere. We need a sharper focus.

Hurley's. It is empty of customers, as I suspected. Community interest is elsewhere this morning.

Teagan is not surprised to find us back in the shop, or to learn that we spoke to Jason. She has eager and undivided attention to bestow on us. In fact, she has more questions for us than we do for her.

I reveal some of what transpired outside Gertie's house, but not enough that she might think we had any motives other than to extend our sympathy to the woman's nephew.

It is plenty, however, to stimulate her urge to contribute. 'People are talking, you know.'

'What are they saying, Teagan?' I ask, having already paid for another ice cream bar and taken the first bite.

'That it couldn't have been anyone from around here. Nobody from Fogo would have done that to Gertie. Like Mother says, she didn't have an enemy in the world. The dirty devil murdered Gertie, then flew off out of here in the middle of the night. It had to be someone who come from away.'

With emphasis on *away*. A stranger. A fly-by-night. Literally.

I won't say it to Teagan now that she's on a roll, but that's rather far-fetched, the flying off bit, without someone know-ing it. Not something you'd get away with, not on this island.

'Whoever done it, he had no love for Fogo Island, that's for bloody sure. Here to say he'd been here. To one of the four corners, all that crap. To the friggin' end of the earth. Then gone. Never to set eyes on the place again.'

Teagan has definitely loosened up. She unleashes even more speculation.

'And where do you think he stayed when he was here? There's only one place. You know that as well as I do. The Inn. Where else?'

'You could be right.' To keep her going.

'I know I'm right. If I was the cops I'd go straight to the Inn and start asking questions.'

'But why?' Mae says. 'Why would some stranger show up at the Inn and then murder some innocent lady in a quilt shop? That doesn't make sense. What's the motive?'

I wouldn't have gone there quite yet. I would have milked it a bit longer to see what else is in Teagan's mind.

Yet Teagan sallies forth, undaunted. 'I thought about that. There's people that don't have a sensible reason. I see it all the time on YouTube. Murdered because some guy wants his Air Jordans. Or his Xbox.'

Or her quilt? Okay. No point in trying to counter that piece of warped logic.

'Mark my words,' she says.

We'll do just that. Mark them as belonging to someone fired up and desperately craving answers. I wouldn't be surprised if she has a thing for Jace, a high-school crush that still lingers.

On our way back to the car, Mae is not quite so dismissive. 'The Inn is worth a look,' she says, 'if for no other reason than to check it off the list.'

She's on her phone and, after a couple of minutes of Mae at her most urbane and affable, has landed us a lunch reservation at the Fogo Island Inn. As far as I know, the Inn only takes reservations if the dining room is not filled with its guests. At peak season she would for certain have been out of luck, but there it is—in an hour we find ourselves seated in its stunning dining room, having confirmed our reservation at the front desk with Loretta, a director of the Inn, the person Mae spoke to on the phone.

The Inn has put Fogo Island on the bucket list of world travellers. The room rates preclude it from appearing on any list I might make, but hey, with Mae paying the bill I'll take the dining experience anytime. Luxuriate in the fine food served in a room defined by its extraordinary banks of floor-to-ceiling windows and iconic white-rope chandeliers.

The innkeeper is Zita Cobb, who, true to her vision, erected a stunning piece of architecture and designed an experience hotel guests will not find anywhere else on the planet. Add to that her unconditional regard for the environment and engagement with the local people, and the Inn reframes the image of what vacation travel can be.

'Your tour guide business is showing through,' says Mae as we look over the lunch menu.

'I admire people with the grit to dream big, outside the box.'

'This place is absolutely outside the box. Look at that view.'

Beyond the windows is a sweeping shoreline rockscape lapped by the frigid North Atlantic. Icebergs. Of course. Crisp, clear northern light glinting off open ocean. Of course.

'No herd of wild caribou traipsing along,' Mae says, 'but come back in mid-winter . . .'

'Of course.'

We both agree it's hardly the place where someone would

come to stay and end up murdering the grey-haired owner of a quilt shop.

Our focus turns to the food that is starting to arrive. Rolls fresh from the oven, nestled in the folds of a woven white tea towel, inside a shallow wooden box, locally made I'm sure, and served with butter dusted with Newfoundland sea salt.

The food and its presentation are very much about this island. Ingredients start with what the sea and land have to offer, a core principle that delivers to me an egg from a hen that hangs out somewhere on Fogo, cooked in a casing of moose sausage, with aioli made with foraged seaweed, resting on a bed of what must be colcannon.

Never heard of colcannon, I admit, until I saw it on the menu. 'What exactly is it?' I enquire of the server after she sets the plate in front of me.

'A traditional Irish dish. A mash of local potatoes and kale.'

The answer comes with a slight Irish accent, which leads me to ask, 'Are you from Tilting, by chance?'

'Yes, I am.' She has been more subdued than I'd expected and now I understand why.

'We're so sorry about what happened.'

'Yes, sir. The poor woman. I have to apologize, we're not ourselves here this morning. We all knew Gertie. Her quilts are everywhere in the Inn.'

By *everywhere* she means in some of the guest rooms. 'Gertie's quilts are not the only ones here, of course,' Mae informs me after the young woman has gone. 'The Inn's quilts are made by quilters from all over the island. It's a hallmark—handmade quilts on all the beds.'

Mae turns to her meal—cod cheek chowder. 'Ummm. So good. And the biscuit—melts in your mouth.'

As wonderful as the food is, I'm distracted. I'm wanting to see Gertie's handiwork, to see at least a room with one of her quilts on a bed. To feel what a guest would feel lying across that quilt and looking out the window at the view beyond. To know if it is at all possible that the experience could plant a craving in the guest's mind to have such a quilt, at all costs.

I don't say anything to Mae. I want her to have time to revel in the Berry in a Bog. And me in the Spruce and Berry Mess, as long as I am able. But my mind returns to the fundamental question: Would a guest of the Inn, some rich but demented stranger, have resorted to murder?

I continue to ruminate over coffee. It, too, is exceptional enough that it should be a distraction.

When Mae takes her final spoonful of dessert, I'm there with the immediate question. 'Do you think there's any way we could get to see one of Gertie's quilts? In the Inn? *In situ?*'

Mae lifts her coffee cup to her lips and, without drinking any, sets it down again. 'There's the person who will give you your answer.'

My line of sight follows hers. Loretta has walked into the dining room.

'Shall we try our luck a second time?'

FOUR POINT STAR

IT'S LIKELY PART of what Loretta does each day, spending time in the dining room, chatting with patrons about their meals, about the Fogo Island they've experienced so far and what they have to look forward to.

She is subdued, as we found her to be at the front desk. Less animated than would be expected on a normal day. Obviously preoccupied with what has happened. I make it the point of entry into conversation as she nears our table.

'We're very sorry. Poor Gertie. What a tragedy.'

It catches her by surprise. 'You were acquainted with Gertie then?' she asks quietly.

I fill her in on how we came to be on the island, only then revealing, 'We're the couple who discovered the body.'

'How dreadful.' She's visibly shaken. 'I still can't believe it. Not Gertie. Not on Fogo Island.'

It establishes a link where there was none before, surreal though it is. We relate our story of the previous evening, avoiding gruesome detail. Yet it adds to her upset, I'm afraid. It is a testament to the personal relationships the staff of the Inn have built up over the years with the quilters of Fogo Island.

In the end a door has been opened to our request. A request that comes best from Mae, given her more intimate link to quilting.

'Over the years Gertie purchased fabric from my store. We would love to see how she chose to use it, in quilts for a place where people from all over the world could admire her handiwork.'

Very nicely put, Mae.

'Would it be possible to visit a vacant guest room that uses one of her quilts?' I ask, gently, sincerely.

Not what the listener would expect of casual diners, but we are something more. We're sharers in a tragedy, likely the worst to befall her beloved island in recent years. Our request gives rise to what I see as her way of consoling us for having endured the unspeakable.

'Please check at the front desk when you finish your meal. I'll see what I can arrange. Thank you for being so respectful of Gertie.'

'Thank *you* very much.'

She draws away. Other diners, who likely know nothing of what has happened, are expecting a lighthearted chat. She moves on.

We get a refill on the coffee, lingering in subdued conversation to allow the time needed for the arrangement at the front desk to proceed and hopefully bring the good news on which our hearts are now set. It does, yes, and more.

Loretta has spoken with Zita Cobb and confirmed it was fine for Loretta herself to lead us on a brief tour of the Inn. As it turns out, the tour has more stops than we could have anticipated—the library, the cinema, the art gallery, the meeting/concert room, the rooftop sauna and hot tubs. We stop briefly at each, admiring the fusion of clean Nordic design and Newfoundland culture. The attention to detail is striking throughout, nowhere more so than at the final stop—the much-anticipated guest room.

The ocean scene through the tall bank of windows is, again, remarkable. It is the natural inclination to linger before it for a moment, trying not to dwell on the adjacent, freestanding bathtub, and the images it brings to the mind.

And then move quickly on to the locally crafted and up-holstered furniture, the specially designed wallpaper with its congregation of caribou in a forest setting, the charming little woodstove to fend off any chill after your partner emerges from the tub.

The true focus is the quilt that is spread across the king-size bed. It leads to another lesson in quilt appreciation from Mae. I listen intently, trusting Gertie's handiwork could possibly offer some clue, no matter how tenuous, to her demise.

'Four Point Star,' Mae informs me. 'Each star made up of four interlocking pieces of fabric, precisely cut, a careful balance of prints and solid colour.'

Got it. I calculate there's at least a couple of hundred stars, arranged in rows, their tips barely touching. Mae looks more closely at where they meet. 'Perfect points,' she notes. Not for my benefit of course. I already know Gertie as a virtuoso of the perfect point, a consummate quilter.

'See how the pattern produces octagonals surrounding the stars. Their contrasting white fabric draws your eye to the stars, making them the focus.'

Definitely.

She continues, 'A sandwich is made of the pieced quilt top, the batting in the centre, and backing fabric. All sewn together, quilted in a pattern stitched over the whole design. The quilt is then bound by sewing thin strips of a coordinating fabric along all four sides. True quilters will machine sew one side, then hand sew the other, as a final personal touch, before attaching a label.'

Lost me partway through.

Loretta turns over a corner of the quilt to expose the label. Hand-stitched to read 'Made by Gertie Pottle on Fogo Island.'

'Beautiful.' That sums it up for me.

'Four Point Star. A challenge for all but the expert quilter.' And that sums it up for Mae.

One final moment of communal appreciation before we depart the guest room and make our way downstairs, back to the front desk.

To be honest, there was nothing in the encounter with the quilt that triggered a connection to the murder. Nothing in the whole tour, in fact, that would lead me to believe the perpetrator had been a guest at the Inn.

'One final thing to show you,' Loretta says, drawing our attention to what is hanging behind her. 'These are a few of the twenty-nine key fobs, all different, one for each guest room, each a cultural artifact or object of local significance, cast in bronze.'

It is original touches such as these that set the Inn apart. I lean over the desk, arms crossed, admiring them.

The fobs not in use are hung individually against dark grey panels. An arresting assembly as it is, and one that must be a work of art when all twenty-nine are hung together. I recognize several of them—a rope coil, a net buoy, a thread spool.

Loretta unhooks one and sets it in my hand. 'Do you know what this is?'

It is flat, like a short ruler, pointed at one end, its interior partly cut away, leaving a thin bit projecting through the centre. Even miniaturized, it is a weighty artifact. I shake my head. 'No clue.'

'A twine needle. For fishermen knitting and mending nets. The twine is wound inside and released as the fisherman works at the net.'

'Very clever.'

But that's not all I'm thinking. In this business when you're talking murder, you're also talking potential weapons. That pointed end of bronze gripped in a fist could do serious damage.

My attention flashes to the remaining fobs. Yes, no doubt about it, there's more than one that in villainous hands could do untold damage to a skull. Leads me to wonder if the stork scissors were a ploy, a distraction, secondary to the real cause of death. Leads me to wonder what the cops found when they examined the other side of Gertie's head, the side lying against the floor.

'I hope you both enjoyed the tour,' says Loretta, by way of bringing it to an end.

'Yes, indeed,' I tell her. 'Thank you very much. It was very kind of you.'

'Was there anything that stirred your interest in particular, Mr. Synard? Any clues, so to speak?'

'Clues?'

She smiles gently. 'You *are* a private investigator.'

Catches me off guard. No point in denying it. 'Yes, as a matter of fact, I happen to be in that line of work, part-time.'

'So I understand. That incident last year, in Trinity. It caused a bit of a stir online.'

I see. Hard to remain anonymous these days. Surprising she would have dug into my background. And so quickly. I have to assume she didn't entirely buy into our reason for wanting to see Gertie's quilt.

Mae steps in. 'Forgive us. Our concern is to find out who murdered the dear woman.'

There's a lot to be said for the upfront, straight-to-the-point approach.

'Wouldn't that be better left in the hands of the police?'

This one I've tackled before. 'In most cases, I would say yes. In this case, because I was on the ground from the beginning, in fact *ahead* of the police, I have a definite sense I can be helpful to their investigation. Time is of the essence.'

'*We,*' notes Mae. 'We can go places. Before the trail runs cold.'

Loretta appreciates Mae's candour, her insistence on her value to the investigation.

Of course Mae is invaluable, as I'm about to say before my chain of thought is suddenly interrupted.

'I do hope the trail isn't leading to the Inn. I see the key fobs have taken your attention. What might you be thinking? A potential murder weapon?'

One step ahead of us again.

'You should know that nobody has checked out of the Inn since yesterday morning,' Loretta informs us.

Which could mean there's a weapon still in the hands of a murderer who hasn't yet checked out.

'The RCMP have already been told that no one from the Inn has left the island and I am about to inform the guests who are due to leave that it is possible they will be interviewed by the police before departing. In any case we have their complete contact information, should it be required. I don't know your thinking, but wouldn't you both agree that it would be foolish in the extreme for some guest at the Inn to commit murder when he or she would be so easily traced?'

She has a point. I step away from the desk, away from the twine needle fob still resting there.

Okay. About time to make a quiet exit. We have work to do.

'Please don't let our key fobs become a distraction, Mr. Synard.'

'Thank you once again. You have been very generous.'

'We did appreciate spending time with Gertie's work,' Mae

inserts. 'She was a gifted quilter. I just love her Four Point Star. She had a wonderful sense of colour.'

'She certainly did, Mae.'

Leave it to quilting talk to alter the mood.

'And did you notice her points, Loretta?'

'Always perfect.'

'Perfect points.'

Dear God. Does the world rotate around perfect points? A woman has been murdered and these people are focused on perfect points.

'Gertie had the soul of an artist,' says Loretta. 'She loved to experiment, to try new approaches to see where it would take her. She had faith in the knowledge that something fresh, something special would come from it. She brought a personal philosophy to her quilt-making, one we could all learn from. Her perfect points were an outward sign of so much more. We will all miss her dearly.'

I follow Mae's lead out the front entrance, with a final raised hand to our guide before the doors close.

'There,' says Mae, as we make our way along the road to the car, 'that went exceptionally well. I don't know about you, but I learned a lot.'

She's made that point perfectly.

ROB PETER TO PAY PAUL

I NEED UNWINDING. I need exercise. I need fresh oxygen infiltrating my brain cells.

'Let's take a hike,' I tell Mae.

'A break from the case?'

'We shouldn't forget our original itinerary.'

'Before murder got in the way.'

'Time to refresh and refocus.'

'I read about a trail along the shoreline in Tilting. Looks very picturesque. Leads to a sandy beach.'

'I'm all for picturesque.'

Let's give it a go. Let's direct our pent-up energy to Turpin's Trail, which starts just next to the Lane House Museum.

And there we find a winding, narrow path that leads to the balding rock of a coastline set against high, bright azure sky and a few wispy trails of cloud. How reassuring. How restorative.

'Off we go.'

'Into the wild and the blue.'

This is what hiking in Newfoundland is all about—an unpredictable coastline dictating your path, be it sandy beach, weathered but accessible rock, or sheer cliff. Impossible to anticipate what awaits the eye over the next incline. One thing you do know—it will be a gift of nature to a receptive soul.

A gift of nature with a bright white, angular, sky-reaching box of . . . a retreat? A hideout? A haven? Whatever it is, it's perched on the shoreline, a cut of modern art on barren rock.

'An artist's studio,' Mae tells me.

'Really?' I knew remote Fogo Island had suddenly been discovered by artists. And I knew studios had been built especially for them. What I didn't know was that one of the studios is a futuristic sanctum that practically kisses the North Atlantic.

'There are four studios, on different parts of the island, all unique in design, all part of the artist-in-residence program. Artists come from around the world to spend a month.'

'Creating?'

'Exactly. Cool don't you think?'

'Especially in winter.'

'Hence the woodpile.'

I see the stacks of drying wood nearby. For a stove inside the studio, given the shiny chimney pipe extending above its slanted roof.

'Totally off the grid.'

Hence the solar panels. 'Very cool.'

We seem to have arrived at an opportune moment. A woman—the resident artist, I would think—emerges from the studio. She has longish greying hair. Mid-fifties is my guess. She's wearing brightly coloured tie-dyed leggings and a chunky, mottled yellow-and-orange sweater. Having spent an eventful few days in Mexico a couple of years back, if I were to judge facial features and fondness for vivid attire, I would say Mexican heritage.

She looks about before connecting to the path that leads

back into town. That means passing by the newly arrived hikers.

As she nears us, it is obvious she is upset. She looks prepared to go past without making eye contact, foreign and unbecoming behaviour if you're in Newfoundland. As we step aside to let her by, I see she's been crying.

'Can we help you?'

Her stride is interrupted and she stumbles slightly before catching herself. The book and binder she has been carrying end up on the moss-covered rock just off the path.

She looks our way. 'I'm okay.' Her breath is heaving as she bends down. She reaches first for the binder.

She's obviously not okay.

'Let me help,' Mae says, retrieving the fallen book. The cover catches her attention.

'I know this book,' she says to the woman. 'I love their work.'

I crane my neck to read the title. *The Quilts of Gee's Bend.* Means nothing to me. But obviously a lot to Mae.

Now upright, the woman doesn't speak as she reaches for the book. She wants only to continue along the path.

Mae is not one to give up easily. 'Are you a quilter then?'

She shakes her head. 'A fabric artist,' she answers quickly, to be done with us.

'What exactly is a "fabric artist"?'

She gives me a disapproving look and moves on.

'You knew Gertie?' Mae calls after her. 'It's awful what happened.'

She turns back to Mae and bursts into tears.

Mae hurries to the woman and without hesitation embraces her. It surprises me what women do when distressed, even if they're strangers. 'Mae,' she says when they finally disengage.

'Octavia,' the woman responds. 'I only just found out. I had my cell turned off so I could concentrate on my project.

When I finally checked my messages . . .'

Mae is full of sympathy. I maintain a physical distance. I maintain a mental one as well.

Stranger in town. Strikes up relationship with the deceased. From the States, by the sound of her voice. Thus, no stranger to violence.

And again, what *is* a 'fabric artist'? What exactly is her 'project'?

We get to that eventually. Once she has unburdened herself to her new soulmate. Given the bond she has going with Mae after three minutes, I can only imagine what it was with Gertie after three weeks.

Really? Because of a shared interest in fabric. Fabric?

Octavia is also, as she now discloses to Mae, 'very interested in the history of quilting in isolated societies.'

'Which means?' I'm dubious, as Octavia notes.

'Such as Gee's Bend,' says Mae. 'And Fogo Island.'

Falling on ignorant ears.

'I'm doing a comparative study as part of my residency,' she says pointedly to me, before turning to Mae. 'Between the historical quilts of Gee's Bend, Alabama, and those of Fogo Island, Newfoundland. Gertie has been a storehouse of information.'

I may consider backtracking, slightly. For now.

Thanks to Mae, Octavia has a better grip on her emotions as she continues along the path and on to the house where she has been boarding for the month. Mae pockets her cellphone, the bonded duo having added each other to their lists of contacts.

The studio, as we have gathered, is only Octavia's workspace. 'She is staying with a family for the full cultural experience,' as Mae puts it.

I understand. Cod, not catfish. Partridgeberries, not peaches.

Fried chicken, not southern fried chicken.

I will admit the female bonding has paid off nicely. I suspect we'll put that cell number to use before long. I have several more questions for the non-quilting, so-called 'fabric artist.'

We continue our hike. The weather has warmed somewhat. In Newfoundland in the latter part of May, that means removing one layer of clothing and tightening the remaining three. That ice-chilled breeze off the saltwater is a tough challenge for the windbreaker, the North Face label notwithstanding.

Still, the route over the mounds of bald rock is undoubtedly picturesque. Tilting at its rugged best.

We've gone so far that a stop is in order, one in which conversation doesn't compete with the wind. I have spied a large, flat slab of concrete a short distance off the trail. It appears to be an abandoned foundation. I have no idea what once stood here.

Of course my smartphone has all the ideas in the world. While I'm waiting for them to show up, I turn the conversation back to the enigmatic Octavia.

'She's far from enigmatic, Sebastian.'

'You got to admit coming all the way from the sun-drenched Southern States to frigid Fogo to study quilts is a bit bizarre.'

Mae shakes her head, smiling indulgently. 'Geography is no obstacle to lovers of quilts and quilting. They take quilting tours to Iceland, quilting cruises to Norway, quilting retreats to Hawaii. You name it.'

'You mean they go to Hawaii and instead of lying on the beach and drinking wild fruity cocktails, they quilt all day?'

'Most of the day.'

'Unbelievable.'

'You're not in the real world sometimes, Sebastian.'

I take that with a grain of salt. 'Besides, your new-found

friend Octavia is not a quilter. She's a quote/unquote "fabric artist."'

Mae continues shaking her head. Fortunately the iPhone has coughed up the info about the abandoned foundation.

'We're on what's called Bunker Hill, site of—get this—the first Ground Radar Early Warning station in the North Atlantic. In the summer of 1942, fifty-two members of the US Army 685th Air Warning Squadron turned up to operate it. Three officers, one doctor, two medical attendants, and forty-six technicians.'

A much-welcomed insertion of undisputed fact. Back on solid ground. 'The antenna stood eighty feet high. The perimeter was protected by barbed wire and seven thirty-calibre machine guns. Patrolled by armed soldiers and K-9 dogs. And— get this—it was the exact same unit that was established at Pearl Harbor!' I take a moment for it to sink in. 'Good God, Mae, we're sitting on a stunning piece of military history.'

She's talking quilting and I'm talking deterring Nazi invasion.

'Did anything ever show up on the radar? Did they ever detect enemy aircraft?'

'It doesn't say. The radar site was absolutely top secret. Even the Fogo Islanders had no clue what was going on.'

Mae is not particularly impressed. Which, to my mind, shows a need to expand her knowledge base beyond the here and now.

'Shouldn't we just focus on the murder? We don't want to be wasting time. Or you're thinking there's some connection?'

'Between?'

'Between the murder and the military history.'

Can't say I'd really thought of that.

'Possibly.'

'Stretching it, don't you think?'

Her mistrust is not healthy. For our relationship, among other things.

'Why don't we ask her?'

'You mean Octavia?'

There's a need to assert myself, maintain control. After all, I'm the one trained for the job. 'Yes, Octavia.'

The mistrust intensifies.

'Text her right now. Set up a meeting. Tell her we have several questions.'

Turning the tables, as it were. I smile pleasantly to help things along. Help transition her reluctance into something positive.

She eases her cell from her coat pocket. 'She's going to wonder what's up.' Nevertheless, Mae follows through. She repockets the cell.

I hear a message ding. That was quick.

Phone eased out again. 'That was quick,' she says.

Good to see we're on the same wavelength.

She reads, 'Meet me in the studio. I'll be there in a half-hour.'

I bite my tongue. Not one scrap of self-satisfaction from me.

In the meantime we have thirty minutes to kill. 'Let's keep walking. Soak up the scenery before we head back. It's bound to be picturesque.' Plus it will give me time to decide what questions to be asking the fabric artist.

The hike eventually brings a change of scenery. Rock gives way to sandy beach, the beach we drove past on the road to Tilting. And the one I read about in the online account of the radar station, though I hadn't told Mae, given her dearth of interest in what I had disclosed up to that point.

It's known as Sandy Cove. This is where the army barracks were situated, where the American GIs spent their time when not manning the guns or the radar station.

Hope they had the forethought to bring swimming trunks. I can picture it—beach towels, Camel cigarettes, Coca-Cola. Young bucks craving female company.

Nothing remains of the barracks, nor anything of the mess hall, rec room, and hospital. There are only the open, grassy fields where they all once stood. I show Mae the picture of the buildings on my phone. Then flick to one of a dozen or so men lounging around the front steps of the barracks. Most in military fatigues, some not. One fellow holding a guitar. Almost all of them looking pleased to be so very far away from the firing lines in Europe and the Pacific.

Her reaction is low-pitched and unmistakable. 'Wow.'

It all comes down to putting a human face on history. A lesson learned from my ex-life as a high-school teacher. I'm smiling, but still managing to keep the self-satisfaction in check.

'Good-looking guys,' she says. 'The local girls must have been bowled over.'

Sweet talk and Juicy Fruit, pristine teeth and Vitalis. Tough competition for the home-grown lads.

She enlarges one section of the picture. 'Interesting,' she says.

Octavia sees us arrive at the studio entrance before we have a chance to knock. She holds the door open.

Her colourful apparel sets her in sharp contrast to the interior space. It's white from floor to angled ceiling, the black wood stove and stovepipe the only exception. Our gaze is directed to the back wall of windows and its broad view to the foreshore, the sea beyond, and a rocky headland in the distance. The architecture has framed a wild, untamed piece of Fogo Island for the visiting artist. Very clever.

'Must be hard to concentrate,' I offer, in an effort to bring a sense of normality to the moment.

Octavia says, 'I work at being disciplined.' Which, to me at least, sounds open to interpretation.

'I know what you mean,' says Mae, whose attention has turned to a table on which is laid a wide array of textiles of various patterns, shapes and textures, some cut and stitched together on a backing stretched within a wooden frame. 'This is marvellous. It really speaks to me.'

But Octavia has more than fabric on her mind. 'I've been in Gertie's shop practically every day since I arrived here. She had me over to her house for coffee. I took her out for meals. Please, what else can you tell me about what happened?'

Of course there is a lot we can tell her. Just how much and in what order is another matter, given her motive for asking, whatever that might be. Interest out of love for a friend? A way of figuring out just what suspicions are out there about who might have done it? Whether non-residents rank high on the suspect list?

I start by coming clean about who we are exactly. She'd find out in time, regardless. And then clam up in reaction to not being told.

It turns out to be no big deal to her. And her reaction no surprise to me, the woman coming from the States and all, where PIs are thick as flies.

What *is* a bit of a deal is the fact that I turned up at the scene of the crime very shortly after it happened.

'The fact is I wouldn't have been there except for Mae. She's the keener as far as quilting goes. I'm the hanger-on.'

A tactic to divert attention away from Octavia thinking I might have her on a suspect list. I can tell that's not quite doing it for her. She needs more.

'Mae has opened my eyes to an art form I'll admit I know little about. How long have you been a fabric artist?' The two words slip out with ease, helping to solidify in her mind that any misgivings I might have about what she does in life have fallen away. That I take whatever is going on within the frame on that worktable to be art (even if it doesn't really 'speak to me').

Octavia, however, has no interest in discussing her creative self. 'Please, Gertie was the dearest human being. Why would anyone ever do such a thing?'

'It's unbelievable, but it happened,' Mae interjects. 'And to be perfectly honest, the perpetrator is more likely to be someone from away than someone who lives here permanently. That's our consensus, given what we know of everyday life on Fogo Island. Unless, of course, the person was deranged. And clearly the RCMP detachment here would be well aware of any resident who falls into that category.'

Octavia's hands come together before her lips in prayer-like gesture. She falls into the ergonomic office chair next to the worktable. 'Oh my God.'

Mae is quick to her rescue. 'There's no need to panic. I'm sure there are lots of people who will vouch for you, if the police start asking questions.'

No *if* about it. 'The police will want to know where you were last evening, say between the hours of five and eight p.m.' Taking the passive route to getting the answers I'm after. A PI tactic, one not easily learned.

'I was right here in the studio, working late. My show at the gallery at the Inn goes up next week.'

'They'll want to know if there is anyone who can confirm that.'

She is having trouble remembering. 'I was so focused on this piece. It's the final one for the show.'

'Not enough to satisfy the RCMP, I'm afraid.'

Suddenly she thinks of someone. 'Jace. Jace came by with

a cold plate. I knew I would be working late so I ordered a cold plate. The firefighters had a fundraiser. I love all the bright colours. Especially the beet salad and the mustard pickles. And the green Jello with grated carrot.'

Way too much information. You could put it down to her nervousness. I'm not so sure. In any case, it needs explanation.

'You mean Jace, Gertie's nephew?' Mae asks, before I have chance. Mae is thinking what I'm thinking—there can't be many Jaces in Tilting.

'I got to know him from spending time with Gertie. He's a volunteer fireman. A lovely young man, always there to help.'

Including delivery of the ubiquitous cold plate, mainstay of outport fundraisers.

'In fact, a cold plate was the inspiration for one of the pieces in the show. I think of the cold plate as a colour palette.'

I must say, the bright pink beet and potato salad are not my favourites. I tend to stick to the ham and turkey slices. Now that I think about it, they make a nice contrast with the red of the partridgeberry sauce. Truth be told, I never pay much attention to the colour combination.

'It takes an artist to fully appreciate a cold plate,' says Mae. I think she is being facetious, but I'm not sure.

I come to my senses. This is all starting to look like a diversionary tactic on the part of Octavia. 'What time did Jason show up here?'

It takes a few moments longer than it should. 'I'm thinking six, maybe six-thirty.'

'Did he stay long?'

'Not really. He had other deliveries to make.'

Doesn't exactly provide much backup for the three hours in question. 'No other visitors? Phone calls? Texts?'

'I FaceTimed Gertie at one point.'

She what? And didn't mention it straight away? 'You Face-

Timed the victim?'

'It wasn't for long. I was fact-checking Rob Peter to Pay Paul.'

She was doing what?

'It's a quilt pattern,' Mae says.

'For the speech I'm giving at the opening of the show. A comparison of the designs used in Gee's Bend and here.'

I see, if somewhat dimly.

'Gertie has been using that pattern for a long time, and her mother before her. In fact she was using it for the quilt she was working on when I called.'

I look at Mae. Really? Gertie wasn't working on Lover's Knot, the quilt thrown over her after she was murdered?

'Are you sure?'

'She turned her phone to show me.'

Rob Peter to Pay Paul set aside to make way for Lover's Knot. Very interesting. Potentially speaks volumes.

'Is that all you talked about?'

'For the most part.'

I need more than that. 'The police will want it all.'

Octavia is reluctant. If she's going to clear herself from any list of suspects, she's going to have to be more forthcoming. Cops don't do well with reticence.

Not something she needs to be told. I'm fully prepared to wait her out.

She holds tight. 'Would either of you like coffee?'

No, not at this point.

Mae looks at her until Octavia meets her eye. 'Did you and Gertie ever speak about genealogy?' Mae says. That came out of nowhere.

Throws me for a loop, but throws Octavia for a bigger one. She takes a deep, concentrated breath, then bursts into tears.

Just the prompt needed for the two women to wrap their

arms around each other once again. Good God, is there no limit to this fabric emotional affinity?

It takes a good two minutes before the pair finally regain control, while I stand to one side, arms folded, wondering where Mae will take it from here, now that she has forsaken every ounce of objectivity in dealing with Octavia. I release a lungful of exasperated air.

'What was his name?' she says to Octavia.

What? What the frig is she talking about? *His name.*

'Luis.'

Luis? What the frig, *Luis*?

'Luis Sanchez,' says Octavia. 'He was from Puerto Rico.'

'He was Gertie's biological father?' Mae says.

'And my grandfather.'

'Which made Gertie . . .'

'My half-aunt,' Octavia says.

I give up. What chunk of reality have I been deprived of?

'Would one of you please clue me in?'

They both do, by turns. Gertie's biological father, the afore-mentioned Luis Sanchez, was a US Army radar technician stationed on Fogo Island during the war. A love affair with one of the local young women resulted in Gertie, although before she was born, father Luis had been reassigned to a radar site in the States. When the war ended a year later, Luis sent money, excited that the mother and child could join him in Brooklyn, where Luis had settled by this time. But Gertie's grandparents in Tilting were fearful of them going and persuaded their daughter it was a dangerous trip, that she would never be happy once she got there. And that ended the relationship with Luis.

'He married my grandmother in 1948,' says Octavia. 'I grew up never knowing anything about this until my Papi passed away, several years after my grandmother. He was ninety and he kept this secret from us all his life. Then after he died, clearing out their house, I found a small envelope of old photographs, tucked away in a dresser.'

'Was this one of them?' Mae opens the photos on her phone and shows Octavia. She nods. Then passes the phone to me. 'It was in a frame on a shelf in Gertie's workroom. You didn't notice?'

Obviously not. It shows a handsome uniformed young man standing with an attractive young woman in a floral summer dress. His arm is around her waist. They are both smiling. In love, one could easily conclude.

The same picture Octavia now shows us from an envelope holding several more. They are small, black and white, with deckled edges, none very sharp, but clear enough to speculate that the couple spent considerable time together. The last picture is of Luis Sanchez and his army buddies, very similar to the photo on the website, the one I showed Mae earlier this afternoon. Octavia shows its reverse side. On it is pencilled "Tilting, Newfoundland."

'Gertie's mother eventually married a local fisherman, and the man raised Gertie as his own. But out of the picture was her birth father, somewhere far away in the States. The whole island was aware of it, even if it was never talked about. And you could see it in her face, of course.'

'I only met her once. She was visiting St. John's and came to the store,' Mae says. 'But I do remember thinking at the time there was something about her features that wasn't typical of an outport Newfoundland woman.'

'You won't believe this, but after I first made contact with her, she went online and started to teach herself Spanish. She wanted to know a few phrases at least for when I finally made it to the island.'

The story swirls around me as I stand there. Outmanoeuvred, somewhat. I have to concede—Mae played it well.

I give credit where credit is due. However, let's separate fact from emotion. 'Gertie never married, I understand?'

'She didn't. Although I doubt it was for lack of opportunity,' Octavia says. 'She was a good-looking woman, even well into her 70s. And clever, as we all know.'

'An outsider because of her background.' That would be my explanation.

'For a while, I thought the same,' says Octavia. 'But getting to know her better, I doubt it. She only ever had good things to say about people. There was never any hint the circumstance of her birth was held against her.'

'She just didn't want to marry,' says Mae. 'Or the right man didn't came along. You know the way it is with men—it's more by luck than judgment.'

Really, Mae?

In that case, your bad luck is in the past. I smile quietly to myself.

'You're right there,' Octavia tells her. 'We all have our stories.'

The two of them share their smiles, pleased with themselves. Yet another bonding moment.

Time to move on, Mae, time to bring Octavia into sharper focus. Time to be dealing in fact.

Time to be a bit more hard-nosed about what, exactly, Octavia is all about. 'Would you say your foremost reason for coming to Fogo Island was to spend time with your half-aunt?'

She's quick to reply. 'Do you mean was my work as a fabric artist an excuse?'

You could put it that way, but I don't. 'Not an excuse exactly.'

'A convenient motive?'

'If you prefer.'

'I wouldn't.' She's turning a bit steely. 'Artists generally don't make a lot of money, Mr. Synard. We rely on opportunities that present themselves. This residency is rigorously competitive. I was chosen on the merits of my work and my research.'

Steely, with the temperature turned up. I am not deterred. In investigative questioning it is often the tactic of the person being questioned to set him- or herself in a superior position.

'Would you mind telling me how you came to be studying the quilt-makers of Gee's Bend in Alabama when you grew up in Brooklyn? Aren't the cultures somewhat far removed?'

'Are you implying that Puerto Rican culture doesn't allow for diversity of academic interest?'

'Not exactly.'

'What then?'

Okay, I'm feeling the heat. But no way am I about to exit the kitchen.

'I would have thought there were a number of academics in the Southern US who were closer . . .'

'I think what he means,' Mae interjects, 'is he's surprised. Purely from an outsider's viewpoint. Not being engaged in the arts.'

I don't need Mae to save my ass. The steam has begun to rise.

'Fabric art and/or quilting might not be my thing, but I take that as an asset, not a liability. I deal in facts, and the fact is someone was murdered, and no one is above suspicion until the stories add up. Emotion is beside the point. Objectivity is the point, people, objectivity.'

Mae hesitates to re-enter the fray. Not so Octavia.

'People? I was more than a person. How about friend? How about half-niece.'

A half-niece wrapped up in her own importance. How about that?

Considerable steam on both sides. Mae inserts herself

finally, as peacemaker.

'Let's call it a day. Octavia has work to do for her show. We have other things that need attention.'

What other things? Her objective is to get me outside and into the open air.

'We'll be seeing you again no doubt,' I say to the fabric artist standing there disgruntled.

Mae moves closer to her. I'm on the way to the front entrance before I have to witness yet another encircling of arms.

When Mae joins me I'm already well on the route back to the car.

I can't contain myself. 'Please don't take this the wrong way, but becoming emotionally involved with the woman is not in the best interests of the case.'

'She did open up.'

'To the extent that it was in her interest to open up. And how much is truth and how much is a play on your empathy? She's first and foremost a suspect.'

'Really? You really think she could brutally murder anyone, let alone a relative.'

'It's possible, yes.'

'Possible, but highly improbable.'

'What about this Gee's Bend bit? You buy into that?'

'Yes. Her husband is originally from Alabama.'

The walk comes to a halt. I hesitate a few seconds to emphasize my point. 'She told you that?'

'He's African American. He's related to one of the quilters.'

'She told you that?' I repeat. Meaning the woman told her but not me.

'As I was leaving.'

Mae can see I'm waiting for more.

'She's an accomplished woman. She believes she shouldn't have to defend her career choice.'

'To me, but not you?'

'I didn't ask. She volunteered the information.'

I'm still waiting for more.

'It's women,' Mae says. 'We have our understandings.'

Understandings? There's a clever choice of words. Let me put that one under consideration.

I do not give in to the impulse to take it further. We walk on.

I wish I could say that was the end of it.

A FLOWER IN WINTER

I DON'T UNDERSTAND women. That's the crux of the situation. That's what it comes down to when I try being objective (and God knows I've been trying for decades). I'm far from a sexist bastard. I'm easy enough to get along with. I'm level-headed. I just need proof. That's my job.

'You're right,' Mae says as we near the car. 'If you think I shouldn't be convinced by Octavia's story, that's your prerogative.'

'We'll just leave it at that.'

She's dying to say more, I can tell.

'Go ahead. What's on your mind?'

'No, I'm good,' she says. Pause. 'Let's go back to the house and open a bottle of wine. We both could use some downtime.'

Best suggestion I've heard all day. 'I'm all for that.'

'Great. Look, the sun is coming out. It's warming up.'

She's right. We dispense with the windbreakers. I put an arm around her shoulder. Isn't entirely spontaneous, but it is sincere. Differences of opinion are healthy in a relationship. Or so they say.

The drive back to our saltbox rental is untarnished by

conversation. A silent exchange of smiles reinforces my comfort level. One hopes that, just as I am doing, she is focusing on what holds us together rather than what draws us apart.

As we approach the house, I notice its twin a short distance to the right of us is now occupied. Someone else catching the pleasures of the early tourist season on Fogo Island. I'm pleased for the owners that business has taken hold. Bodes well for a profitable summer.

And by the sound of it the folks have brought along a dog. I hear the barking as we exit the car and I retrieve the key to our abode. Lovely. I'm missing the excited bark of a mutt.

And not only that, but the bark is as robust and distinctive as that of the fun-loving Gaffer. That charming 'arf' with an 'h.' 'Harf, harf, harf.' And I thought it was only Gaffer who brought that special canine accent to his bark.

When I turn to catch a glimpse of the dog, what I see is the mutt bounding over the rocks straight toward me, leash dragging behind. The mutt even looks like Gaffer.

What the hell, it *is* Gaffer. Clambering at my legs. I bend down and he jumps to meet my face, licking it madly.

And into my blurred sightline comes his handler.

My son. What the hell?

'I should explain,' says Mae.

'Dad! Hey, man!'

He wraps his arms around me. The befuddled father reciprocates.

Nick releases me. 'Surprise!'

Understatement.

'I was of two minds whether to tell you,' says Mae.

And slowly coming into view are a woman, her thin dress catching the breeze, and a man, his bare chest doing the same. They approach over rocks from the shoreline, mirage-like, as if they've emerged from the sea.

My head jerks slightly and my mind recalibrates. Not primal creatures, but ex-wife Samantha and bedfellow Frederick, in open defiance of the temperature.

Disappointment. I preferred the first storyline.

Samantha waves her hand tentatively in the air as the reality takes hold and the distance to their opening lines wastes away. Frederick extends his hand on the final few steps and I have no choice but meet him halfway.

'Good to see you,' he says.

Indeed. Samantha is somewhat less jovial, not quite concealing her awkwardness. A smile of seeming sincerity will have to do.

'I left it as a surprise,' offers Mae.

An explanation is obviously forthcoming. I fail to see any reason for delay. The width of my smile is becoming a strain.

'Samantha and I thought,' says Mae, 'wouldn't it be good fun for all of us to meet up for a couple of days. Away from St. John's. A fresh environment to experience together.'

Really? New significant other and ex-wife have a convivial tête-à-tête, only to have it result in a sudden awakening as to the potential benefit of the respective couples joining forces (together with the teenage son of two of them + dog)?

'Great idea, eh Dad?' says the teenage son. The dog barks.

'Terrific.' That would be me. My enthusiasm is pronounced if not overwhelming.

'Let's all get together after supper for a bonfire on the beach,' injects Mae, seemingly relieved by what has unfolded so far.

'Yes!' declares Nick.

'We'll bring the marshmallows,' says Mae.

'And we'll bring the weenies,' chimes in Frederick, right on cue. Although I suspect 'weenies' didn't come easily to his lips. He's determined to play his part.

Can I dampen this exuberant display? No.
We part ways at that.

You would think I'd be all over this scenario. A sincere attempt
on the part of the woman in my life to jump-start a revision
of my relationship with my ex and her pumped-up paramour.
Sincere but misguided.

We're finally alone inside the house. 'That was painful.' It is
the best I can do.

'I'm sorry if I put you in an awkward position,' she says.
She sits on the couch, but gets up right away, retrieves a beer
from the refrigerator, sits at the table, twists off the cap, then sits
back on the couch again. She's not sure what to be doing with
herself.

'It is well-intentioned,' she says.

No doubt. Well-intentioned but misguided. 'Did you see
that guy? He manscapes. Not a fucking hair on the chest.'

She laughs out loud. On edge. Rattled still.

'I'm serious. The guy's fifty-something and he needs to be
doing that? Give me a fucking break. Serious self-image problem
if you ask me.'

'That's beside the point. Samantha and Frederick are making
an effort to meet you halfway and you're hung up on the guy's
chest hair?'

Well, now. Low blow.

I go looking for Scotch.

'I'm sorry. You're not hung up on his chest hair.'

Sorry, but it's already been stated.

'So you think it's *my* problem?'

'It's *our* problem. And it's one that needs to be addressed.
Sebastian, listen to me. If I'm going to be in a relationship with
you, then we all need to get over our resentments and move on.
I've made a point of connecting with Samantha. She admits

she's been as stubborn as you are in not putting the past aside. We're all adults. We can all do with being a bit more magnanimous.'

Magnanimous. My faults at least sound literate.

So. Now there's a second person rattled. The person sitting in the armchair across from her. The Scotch goes down as if it were water.

'If for no other reason than Nick.'

Another drink of Scotch. More water.

'He's trying his best . . .'

I hold up my hand. I get the message. I don't need a lecture.

I'm still not making eye contact. Mae gets up and goes in the kitchen. In time there is a rattle of pans. She's making something for supper. While I stew.

It's not that simple. I can't just out of the blue decide to forget everything that's gone on. I can't just slam the book on the past and say to hell with it, here I am, the new amicable me. There's too much firmly embedded in my craw.

The custody arrangement at the top of the list. Nick getting to spend every second weekend with me. Two goddamn days in fourteen—that's it. The rest of the time at his mother's place, whether he wants to or not. All because Samantha bullshitted the judge into thinking Nick needed a regular routine in the house he grew up in. That she would be a more stable influence. Give me a fucking break.

The ink on the divorce papers was hardly dry and along came muscle-bound Frederick to play pseudo-dad to my kid. *My* kid, not his.

'I hadn't realized you resented him so much,' Mae says over supper. Bonus points for determination.

More bonus points for zeroing in on deal-breaker *numero uno*.

She stops there. Treading very carefully. Wisely focusing on the nondescript stir-fry, unsalvageable by the Sauternes.

She's hoping I will pick up the ball and run with it. I'm not in the running mood.

I clean up from supper while Mae reclaims the couch to sip wine and dabble with her phone.

Eventually her voice penetrates the domestic daze. 'I had a text from Octavia. Do you want to hear it?'

The other current drama in my life. Luckily there's more than one section to my brain. 'Sure.'

'Thank you both for your understanding. Today has been very difficult, as you will appreciate. If I can be of further help, please get in touch.'

'Good to know,' I say. Meeting Mae halfway. Clear indication I'm not a total cynic. Given that the text is basically useless. The latter thought I keep to myself.

'Wait. There's a second one.' Pause. 'I felt Gertie could be an artist in her own right. I encouraged her to try designing a quilt pattern. She did. She called it A Flower in Winter.'

Here we go, more quilt talk. 'All yours.'

Deferring to Mae. A nod toward reconciliation. Besides, I have no clue if Octavia's scrap of information has any significance.

'And she sent a picture. Looks like it was taken in the back room at the shop.'

One assumes some days prior to the murder. Winter not quite over. Flowers in desperately short supply.

'Quilters love their flowers,' says Mae, her voice edging in the direction of buoyant.

'Good to know.' There is the risk of sounding disengaged. I stroll to the couch and sit near her.

She enlarges the photo for a close-up of the quilt. 'Could be a variation on Winter Flowers.'

Why not? Stranger things happen in the quilting world, I'm sure.

'Let's see.' She googles 'flower in winter' and goes to Images. 'Love it,' she murmurs, finding something in her scrolling to catch her attention.

She bypasses the fabric patterns for now, which only goes to show there's life beyond quilting. It looks like one of those posters of inspirational sayings. Equally forgettable.

'An old man in love is like a flower in winter,' she reads, adding, 'a Portuguese proverb.'

'Such poetic souls, the Portuguese.'

She taps me playfully on the thigh. 'I think it's sweet.'

Not so sure about the sweet, but I did like the tap. A playful love tap, I want to think.

I stretch an arm to the back of the couch and around her shoulders. She sets the phone aside. She leans my way.

'I'm sorry. I should have talked to you first.'

'No harm done.'

'Really? I hate you being mad at me.'

'I'm not mad.'

'Disappointed.'

'Let's not talk about it. It's done now. We'll just make the most of it.'

What I mean by 'making the most of it' I have no idea. Sounded in control. Sounded like we're capable of surviving this bump in the road.

She rubs her hand along my thigh. Then looks directly at me and kisses me sweetly on the lips.

I'm stirred. My other arm reaches across and draws us tighter. My lips resume where she left off, with an added gush of anticipation.

A loud knock on the door. 'You guys ready? We got the weenies!' Accompanied by an excited bark.

Lovely. Impeccable timing on the part of my progeny.

And with that he opens the door and sticks his head in,

while Gaffer slips past and into the room. The mutt leaps to the couch and entangles himself between us. In all of two seconds. The eroticism has vanished.

Mae has a fondness for Gaffer. Fortunately. My own fondness just took a hit, but then again he is my unrelentingly faithful companion. Lust I put to one side for the time being.

The full Nick has made his appearance. He's looking particularly long-limbed, edging even more precipitously toward his father's height. With luck, I'm good for another few months.

'Hi, pal. What's up?'

'Sorry, did I interrupt something?' A slight sporting emphasis on the 'something.'

Better ignored. 'You're wondering about the marshmallows.'

'We're all down by the water. Fred's got a great fire going.'

Fred has, has he.

I catch myself. Promise myself to up my magnanimity. (Might have trouble saying it, but I can think it.)

'We'll be right there.'

'You bring Gaffer. He's been begging to spend time with you guys.' Nick hangs his leash on the back of the nearest chair and makes his exit.

Don't doubt it for a minute. Gaffer always excelled at being a third wheel.

'I'll have to go to a store to get marshmallows,' I say to Mae. 'I didn't pack any.' Since they're the ultimate in empty calories I could do without.

'I did.'

Thinking ahead, one assumes. What's a relationship-repairing campfire without marshmallows?

Gaffer proves to be the diversion needed at this point. The rambunctious mutt, who hasn't spent time with his main man in all of two days, has decided he wants to play chase.

He scampers around the place, racing from room to room, then stops abruptly in front of me and yelps, daring me to chase after him.

Which I do. As if I have a choice. Gaffer being the one to love me unreservedly, no questions asked. Who, when I finally collapse on the couch, bounds up and onto my chest, licking my face in a torrent of thank yous.

Mae stands aside, chuckling at it all. The bag of marshmallows in her hand looks eager to play its part.

The campfire offsets the nocturnal chill, to say nothing of its contribution to the thaw in our relationships.

The two couples are bundled in folding beach chairs. Given it's not yet June, one pair shares a red plaid wool blanket, the other a multicoloured quilt.

'You made it yourself?' says Samantha.

'It's nothing. Leftover scraps.' Even I know it took endless hours of work.

Downplaying is good. Maintaining modesty about our respective fields of endeavour is good. Focusing only on what doesn't generate divergent opinions—perfect. That would be the weather, the location of hiking trails, the opening hours of restaurants. All neutral and conducive to good-natured, if sluggish, chit-chat.

Not only that, but Mae had the foresight to fill a Thermos with hot water, Captain Morgan Spiced Rum, honey, and lemon.

Its effect is twofold. It both warms the body and dilutes the paranoia. Added to that is the distraction provided by Nick, watchdog of the fire, doling out marshmallows, one to each of us in turn, roasted as per our individual requests. I go for the thoroughly charred, then discard the black crust so only the centre is left to force down.

The real watchdog is, of course, Gaffer. He lies flat in my lap, so transfixed by the flames he has no interest even in licking the marshmallow bits stuck to my fingers. At the smell of roasted wiener he re-energizes. Undoubtedly it fits into numerous questionable food groups, but hey, what's more enticing than a burned hot dog on a stick?

Actually, there is something more enticing, according to Nick. Something called a squid dog. 'I discovered it online,' says Nick. The World Wide Web teems with creative thinkers. I can't wait.

He proceeds to demonstrate the simple yet revolutionary technique. With his Swiss Army knife (from Dad, two Christmases ago) he slices the wiener in half, to within an inch of the butt end. Then skillfully turns the wiener ninety degrees and makes two more cuts down to the same point. Insert stick in butt end, and there you have it—squid dog formed by the fire-curled wiener ends. Who knew?

Gaffer is excited, to say the least. Everyone else takes a pass in favour of Nick presenting the squid dog to the actual dog. Gaffer's campfire experience will be long remembered.

As will ours. You might say it stems from my answer to one innocent question.

'So,' says Frederick, 'what have you been up to since you got here?'

Previous to my entry into the campfire fold, I spent significant time debating what my answer would be to this very question, or any variation of it, since I knew it would only be a matter of time before it would rise up and descend on me in the night air.

Better stated, from my perspective: What have I been up to that I want to disclose? My trepidation, of course, stems from thoughts of a scenario where Inspector Olsen is gung-ho to insert himself in what I consider *my* investigation. (Or, rather *our* investigation, i.e., mine and Mae's.)

'Sightseeing, hiking, eating . . . you know.'

'You heard about the woman who was murdered?'

That was quick. Dive straight in, why don't you.

'It was all the talk on the ferry,' adds Samantha.

Of course it was.

I glance at Mae. She remains tight-lipped, choosing to let me set the boundaries.

'We did hear about it,' I tell them. 'Very sad.'

'It was tourists from St. John's who found the body, apparently.'

'Apparently.'

'It's early in the tourist season,' Olsen says. 'Can't be that many around.'

'I wouldn't say.'

He bypasses me and looks directly at Mae. 'Even fewer with an interest in quilting.'

I cut in from the side, 'You would think.'

'And with a partner who wouldn't tell those waiting outside the quilt shop what had happened,' remarks the inspector, pointedly calm. But then adds, as if it were an afterthought, 'Before driving away in a red Toyota.'

I respond with much more gusto. 'Really? You know red Toyotas—common as dogshit these days.' A bit of crude humour to yank him off his game.

Only Nick laughs. The kid pipes up, 'No offence, Gaffer.'

I laugh along with him.

Olsen is not beyond chuckling himself. Not without, I will note, an undercurrent of cynicism.

I glance at Mae once again. Eyes wider than normal. Eyebrows raised.

Where to take it from here? I could continue the bluff. Play the innocence game for all its worth, for as long as I can keep it up without losing all credibility.

Which is not likely much longer.

Or cave to his tactics and look the bigger man, primed to go head-to-head with the self-assured, well-seasoned Inspector Olsen?

I smile broadly. 'Almost got you, Fred.' Calculated pause. 'Meet the couple who just happened upon the crime scene.' I lay an open hand in Mae's direction. Then draw it back to pair with the other hand, both upraised in front of me. 'What can I say? Chance. Pure chance.'

Neither Frederick nor Samantha knows quite how to respond.

Not so Nick. 'Wow, Dad! Awesome timing! In on the ground floor. Amazing.'

I'm tempted to give him a wink and a nod, but that would strain my professionalism, which, at this juncture, I must maintain at all costs. Still, I can't be anything but thrilled to see Nick jump so quickly into my camp.

'Of course, except for Mae, we wouldn't have been going to the shop in the first place. Thank God for quilting.'

Which knocks Frederick further off his game. I'm no longer the only player. Mae has just been called into action.

Her voice is a tad less effusive than mine. 'It *was* pure chance that we showed up when we did. And it was gruesome, in the extreme.' Frederick and Samantha can't help but note how well we complement each other.

'It must have been awful,' says Samantha.

I like it. The females echoing each other. Another roadblock in Frederick's path to victory.

'So, Sebastian,' he says, 'you've injected yourself into the investigation. Good on ya.'

Good on ya? What's with that?

What's his angle? Where's the payoff? Classic good cop/bad

cop? There's no hiding the skeptic in me. My eyebrows are on the rise.

'No, really, give it all you got. I'm just glad I'm on holiday. Thankfully, Inspector Bowmore has no idea I'm here.'

That would be the aforementioned Ailsa Bowmore of the RCMP provincial headquarters in St. John's. In the past she has teamed up with Frederick of the Royal Newfoundland Constabulary, calling on his criminal investigative expertise for an extra workout.

'Yes, thankfully.' On that much at least we see eye to eye.

'Just want to assure you I'm out of the picture,' he reiterates. I think I believe him.

'No mixing business with pleasure,' Samantha interjects.

Spare me the intimate detail, Samantha. Life is too short to have such images of my ex-wife in my head.

Mae's eye catches mine. She has chosen not to chip in. Not surprising, given our own business/pleasure ratio.

Not only that, but the slight lull in the conversation presents Samantha with the perfect opportunity to pivot.

'I've been thinking that Nick and Gaffer would love to spend the night with you guys.' The boy and dog, it is to be noted, are for the moment wandering the beach, conveniently out of hearing range.

She would have me believe this is a gesture of goodwill on her part. And not an opportunity to frolic without having to worry about how soundproof their bedroom walls might be.

'I think that's a great idea,' says Mae. It's the hint of reconciliation she's been desperately hoping for.

What choice do I have? He who regularly complains about not getting enough time with his son. No choice but to agree. And kick to one side any thoughts I might have had about an amorous entanglement of my own.

Time to call it a night, I'm thinking, before Samantha's

mind veers off into an even more self-serving direction.

But in Mae's mind of course the night is still young. The hot toddies have only partially lived up to their promise. A stiffness lingers around the campfire. No sign as yet of the relaxed, jocular chit-chat that she had been counting on.

'Anyone for a game of Twenty Questions?' I inject. 'How about a few verses of "Kumbaya"?'

From my experience of campfires, humour definitely has its place. Apparently, not my version.

Mae's is more calculated. 'I must tell you what happened to me last week,' she says. 'I've never been so embarrassed.'

Ah, here we have it—bait for a round of most-embarrassing-moment stories. Self-deprecation—always good at loosening up the pretentious among us. It's a time-honoured path to congeniality.

'Yes!' declares Nick, who has just rejoined the soon-to-be merry group. 'I love these!' As does Gaffer apparently. He raises his head and yelps in agreement.

Mae relates the story of arriving late for a meal at the classiest restaurant in St. John's, handing her coat to the receptionist and entering the dining room, only to discover she had forgotten to take off her apron before leaving her house. The grease-stained apron that now covered her evening dress. 'I was mortified,' she reiterates.

Small stuff really. And likely the apron was intricately quilted. I would give it a six out of ten.

Samantha jumps in with unrestrained eagerness, which surprises me. 'Years ago we were in the lineup at Tim Hortons in Clarenville. Suddenly Sebastian started shaking his foot, as if he could feel something inside his pants leg.'

I'm no longer surprised.

'And what should fall out on the floor but a pair of pink panties.'

'Belonging to you,' I point out.

'They got caught up in the dryer and somehow you hadn't noticed,' she counters. 'All eyes in the lineup turned our way. Talk about embarrassed.'

'At least they were clean.'

My quip prompts a groan from Nick.

'Sebastian picked them up and slipped them in his pocket, as if nothing had happened.'

I catch a slight smile from Olsen, followed by an equally slight nod. Do I detect admiration for my casual retrieval of the panties, that show of virile self-control under stress? I nod back. The adult males have a point of connection.

But stop. Let's analyse this. Samantha's anecdote is more about me embarrassing her than it is about anything she did to embarrass herself.

Which again demonstrates her willingness to lay blame where it doesn't belong. As if I'm somehow responsible for static cling.

Of course I can't pursue the point and risk the congeniality (real or otherwise) of the moment. Mae looks at me, with the expectation that I will maintain the chummy momentum and offer up a story of my own.

'I'm thinking the incident at Tim Hortons will do for me, too. We were both embarrassed.'

'C'mon, Dad, don't be a spoilsport.'

No, Nick, at this point in the game, I can do without your encouragement, as buddy-buddy as it is.

I smile and keep my cool.

Olsen steps in. 'I have one.'

There you go. Olsen bright-eyed and bushy-tailed when you least expect it.

But before he has the chance to enthrall us with whatever a hard-boiled senior inspector of the RNC considers embarrassing, we hear a vehicle tearing along the access road, jamming to a stiff stop, its headlights glaring down on us.

The vehicle's door bangs shut and the headlights dim to nothing.

'I'm looking for Sebastian,' someone calls to us.

'You found him.'

'It's me, Jace,' he calls back.

I head his way, leaving Mae to enlighten the others on the young man behind the commotion.

'Jason, how's it goin'?'

There's enough ambient light to see that it's not going well.

'I got a question.'

I hope it's worth the intrusion.

'What's a "sewciopath"?'

'A what?'

He spells it. 'A takeoff on psychopath, right?'

After shaking my head to rearrange the brain cells, I say, 'I guess. Sociopath, more likely.'

'Never heard of it. Sounds even worse.'

'Jason, what the frig are you talking about?'

'We were at Growlers Ice Cream Shop in Joe Batt's, right, inside, waiting in line, right, when this missus shows up in this sweatshirt that says "I'm a sewciopath." Under a drawing of what looked like a sewing machine. Hard to tell for sure with her boobs. And then under that, in smaller letters—get this— "on the road to recovery." It hit me—Jesus, either she don't have a fuckin' clue that Aunt Gertie has been murdered, or she doesn't give a shit 'cause she's off her fuckin' rocker.'

The fellow's grip on reality is in free fall. He's desperate for any scrap of anything that might lead him to his great-aunt's killer. I feel sorry for the poor bugger. His heart is in the right place. I play along, out of sympathy.

'Who's the "we"?'

'Me and Teagan. From Hurley's. She knows you.'

'I see.' And what else I see is that Teagan has made her move on Jace.

'We got talking, you know, about what happened. She had some ideas and I had some ideas. Like they say—two heads are better than one.'

'You had no notion who it might be, in Growlers?'

'Not a fuckin' clue.'

But determined to find out.

'We waited outside, lapping into the partridgeberry-jam-tart ice cream, until out she marls, and right on over to her SUV. Takes a mouthful of ice cream, gets inside, does a U-turn, and she's gone, like a bat out of hell.'

'Before she finished her ice cream?'

'But not before Teagan got her licence plate number.'

Speaking of whom, the store clerk emerges from Jason's pickup and saunters into position next to him.

'Heard my name.'

'The licence plate,' prompts Jason.

'Got a pen?' she says to me. 'All I had was lipstick.'

A PI is never without a pen and in this case also his classic leather-bound notepad.

Teagan stretches her forearm, turns it ninety degrees as Jason flicks on his phone's flashlight. She dictates the six characters—three letters followed by three numbers. Typical of Newfoundland and Labrador plates.

'Yellow Kia SUV,' says Jason. 'Not from Fogo, I guarantee you that.'

I believe him. A fellow his age, forever on the go, he likely knows every vehicle on the island.

'Figured you can find out who it belongs to?' he says. 'A private investigator and all.'

'Not so easy as it sounds. Privacy laws.'

There's a pause, their disappointment obvious.

'But I'll see what I can do.' It's enough to satisfy them. For the moment.

They're not about to leave it at that. They have more on their collective minds. 'We've been thinking.'

I can hardly wait. And now I have someone to share in the response. Mae has made her way up from the beach, curious about what's going on.

'Hi,' says Teagan immediately, with a broad, welcoming smile. It seems the bond between them, initiated at Hurley's, has crystallized.

If Mae is surprised by the pairing of Jace and Teagan, she doesn't show it. Women seem to have this instinct about potential matches.

'What's happenin'?' asks Mae, keeping it casual.

'We've been thinking,' Jason says again. 'The four of us should team up.'

Okay, let's nip this in the bud.

'You need us,' says Jason, 'if you're going to get anywhere with the investigation. The both of us—born and bred on Fogo Island. Knows it like the back of our hands.'

He has a point, a dubious one. One that will probably drag us down multiple dead ends, soaking up valuable time. The 'sewciopath' sweatshirt incident being prime example number one.

'Sounds promising to me,' Mae injects.

Here we go again. Leap headfirst into the decision-making process without consultation. Mae's naïveté still in full view. I take a deep breath.

'What do you think, Sebastian?' she adds. After the fact.

A prolonged look of indecision tempered by an attempt at a smile.

'How about you come by for coffee in the morning?' Mae

says to the other two. 'We'll do a deep think. Have you got time?'

'I'll make time,' says Jason. I detect a spurt of adrenaline.

'The shop is closed on Sundays,' Teagan chimes in.

'Perfect. We'll get on it early. You're good for eight o'clock?'

Everyone is. That would include me, given I have little choice in the matter.

So there we have it. The band of four officially formed and geared up for their first 'deep think.' Three of the four chomping at the bit.

Jace and Teagan depart, spitting a little less gravel than when they arrived.

I'm left shaking my head. I tell Mae the bit about the sweatshirt and the lipsticked licence plate number, expecting amusement equal to my own.

Instead, she takes hold of my arm and leans into my shoulder. 'You never know,' she says.

'You're kidding.'

'What have we got to lose?'

A lot. No comment.

And now the campfire companions need our attention. They are charged with curiosity, of course, but only breezy, uninhibited Nick is game to put it into words. 'What the heck was that all about?'

Specifics are best avoided. 'A couple of sources reporting in.'

'Sources?' says Nick. 'You mean you have those guys like working undercover?'

'We'll leave it at that.'

'Wicked.'

I can do without the 'wicked.'

Frederick is amused, without doubt. I give him credit for not showing it.

Samantha is less restrained. 'Are you sure you know what

you're getting yourself into?'

Really, Samantha? Your level of confidence in your ex-spouse is astounding.

'Sebastian knows what's what.'

An infusion of support by none other than Frederick, the man himself, the spousal equivalent. Much appreciated, I will add.

'Experience is a great teacher,' inserts Nick. Pulled from a list of his father's rejoinders normally directed at him. He hands me a thumbs-up.

'We're good,' adds Mae enthusiastically. 'Everything's under control.'

The confidence boosting is driven by a majority, it would seem. Not that I needed it. Thank you very much.

'Just don't drag Nick into it.' Samantha again. Prompting recall of Nick's participation in his father's (and, as she well knows, Frederick's) encounter with the criminal element during a previous case.

'No worries there,' I tell her, shaking my head. It's ridiculous for her to even be thinking it would come to that.

Nick says nothing. The lad is savvy enough to keep his mouth securely sealed. It does twist oddly, doubtless in an effort to keep from smiling.

'Anything I can do to help, let me know,' says Frederick.

I'll take that at face value.

'Not my jurisdiction, but if there's anything . . .'

'Thanks.' (. . . But no thanks.) 'We're good.'

'What about the licence plate number?' says Mae.

Yes, what about the licence plate number? She's not suggesting . . .

'Perhaps Frederick could put in a request . . .' Her voice trails off as she catches my eye.

'You need owner identification?'

Nothing's going to slip past you, Frederick. 'Not really. It's not important.'

'You're sure? It only takes a phone call.'

'I think we should,' says Mae. 'Just to be on the safe side.'

Once again let Mae have her way. And let Frederick do his good deed for the day.

The notebook is retrieved, the number duly produced.

'Leave it with me,' Frederick says.

I sit mute. Let them take the remainder of the evening in whatever direction they want it to go. I'll just pour myself a Scotch and smoulder in silence.

The atmospheric temperature (as well as the communal one) seems to have dropped significantly. The wool blanket and scrap quilt are no longer doing the trick. Two of the four adults don't have Laphroaig Quarter Cask to warm them. Pity. When I retrieved the bottle from the house, I did bring extra glasses, and set them out for anyone to pour a dram of their own. Frederick hesitated but did succumb.

'I still don't know how you can drink that stuff,' says Samantha. She never did understand Laphroaig.

I smile, then switch back to muted. From what I surmise, if Frederick does drink Scotch in her presence, it is of the insipid, characterless variety.

Nick has furry Gaffer bundled in his arms but even that isn't enough to keep him warm. 'Bit nippy,' he says, rubbing his hands together. 'I think I'll go inside with Gaffer and chill out.'

Euphemism for a text session with his buddies back in St. John's. 'Say hi to Kofi for me.'

'Your bedroom is upstairs,' Mae calls to him. That would be one of two in the house, sharing a wall with our own.

The conversation resurges slightly but fails to regain much momentum. Soon the tolerance for the temperature drop becomes too difficult to fake. Both couples rise and prepare to retreat to their properties.

'Good night, all,' says Mae. Followed by a robust chorus of good nights. We prove very good at remaining civil to the end.

Back inside Mae seems willing to forego any discussion/potential disagreement on how the evening went. I'm all for that. Let's just pack it in for the night and quietly find our way upstairs.

We've only just slipped between the posh, pleasure-seeking white sheets when I swear I hear the odd dog sounds that Gaffer makes when he has a vivid dream.

A wall as soundproof as chicken wire.

I'm not a particularly quiet partner when aroused. I like to vocalize. At least that's what they tell me.

'Let's just snuggle,' whispers Mae.

Really, Mae? That's a plausible alternative?

'Snuggling has its own delights. Sex isn't everything.'

Practically speaking, possibly. I'm far from practical. I'm in need.

Before I come up with a soundless second choice, her arm across my chest relaxes, goes indifferently limp.

She's fallen asleep.

MORNING GLORY

SHE'S UP AND showered when I've only reached the stage of sitting at the side of the bed, eyes adjusting to daylight.

With a couple of additional senses in order, I detect humming blended with the sound of a table being set, blended with the aroma of what are undoubtedly freshly baked muffins.

An aroma so powerful that it draws Nick and Gaffer down the stairs ahead of me. I'm still rifling through my overnight bag, searching for something to cover my unrewarded nakedness.

Not to say that when I do descend the stairs I'm not the chipper companion to all assembled. Including the couple that comes knocking at the door before I'm halfway through the coffee Mae handed me when I stepped into the kitchen.

I check the time. Ten minutes before scheduled arrival. Nothing if not eager to set their investigative wheels in motion.

I take it upon myself to answer the door. 'Good morning, folks. Come in. There's coffee on the go, and I hope you're good with cheesy zucchini muffins. Mae's specialty.'

For which she brought all the ingredients, apparently.

She's thought ahead, as she is inclined to do, having anticipated extra people during our weekend alone. And a dog hanging close by, who expects a tidy bit of muffin to eventually drop to the floor.

I introduce Nick. He is naturally intrigued by the duo, especially Jason, who, try as he might, can't repress his eagerness to embrace his new role.

'This is the way I got it figured.' His opening line would indicate he's probably not had a good night's sleep, with a head running wild with possible directions for the investigative 'team.' A sizable chunk of muffin only boosts his enthusiasm.

'Before you start, a note of caution,' I insert, in an attempt to curb the naïve faith in his abilities. 'Don't limit your theories too early in the game, Jason. Put them all out there for consideration.'

'Exactly,' he says. 'Great minds think alike.' He plunges ahead. 'Like I was saying, this is the way I got it figured. The killer is definitely not from Fogo. Agreed?'

'Agreed,' chimes in Teagan, decidedly on cue.

Ignoring everyone else, he continues. 'But—and this is important—he's still here on the island.'

He looks directly at me, as if he expects me to dismiss it outright. He holds up his hand before I have time to open my mouth.

'Here because if he boards the ferry the cops might start asking questions, put him on a list, and if doesn't make the return trip they'll get suspicious. Instead—lie low on the island, but not too low because then people here will get suspicious.'

'Makes perfect sense to me,' says Teagan.

No surprise there.

'The man's got to eat,' says Jason. 'He's got to show up to buy groceries, right?'

Not about to argue that point.

'This is where Teagan comes in,' he says, nodding in her direction. 'Teagan, you want to take it from here?'

Of course she does. 'On the island you got Hurley's, you got Miller's, and you got the biggie, Foodland. Hurley's I got covered. What we're figuring is we set up meetings with the other two, lay out a list of what to look for in a killer who is trying to act normal and can't pull it off.'

'Good strategy?' Jason says to me.

What can I say at this point without offending them? They mean well, they just haven't got a clue.

'What about the woman buying ice cream, the one in the sweatshirt?' asks Mae, in an attempt to relieve the pressure.

'Still on the table,' says Jason. 'And Octavia, the artist missus—still on the table. Like Sebastian says, don't limit your theories. Put them all out there.'

'We got another one,' says Teagan.

I can't wait.

'Buddy, whoever he is . . .'

That would be killer, I assume.

'Buddy gets it in his head to set the cops off on the wrong track. So after he done it, he starts spreading rumours. You know, about Gertie.'

'Rumours?'

'You know, like she must have done something to some-body if someone wanted to kill her.'

That's as clear as it's likely to get.

'So that's another thing to be looking out for,' she says.

Buddy, the killer, spreading rumours. I get it. I can't help but smile. Not offensively of course. Mae does the same.

My cell rings. I couldn't be more thankful. I check the screen. It's Olsen. Still thankful. I move to a more private location.

'I have the info on the vehicle.' In the flurry of theories

coming at me it had slipped my mind.

'The yellow Kia SUV is registered with a Rose Tizzard of Change Islands.'

Really. Lots of Tizzards in Newfoundland.

'Did the vehicle have a previous owner?'

'It's less than a year old. She's the sole owner.'

Once past the name, the real point of interest positions itself. Change Islands. Owner not from Fogo but its neighbour.

'Thanks very much. Every bit of information helps.' No point in being too effusive. What he's sent my way might just prove useless. A 'sewciopath' living on Change Islands. Just what do I do with that tidy bit of information?

I tell the teammates for starters. There's no avoiding it. They will have to know.

Jason is flat-out flabbergasted. 'Unbelievable. Someone on Change Islands buying a yellow Kia.'

Of course he knows people from Change Islands. Enough at least to form a very definite opinion about the car-buying habits of its general population.

He thinks some more. 'Unless it's a mainlander. Moved in there. Fed up with Toronto. Shows up in Change Islands. Figured they found the Promised Land. Can't figure it myself.'

Nor can I. 'Her name is Rose Tizzard.'

'Holy Jesus!'

That sums it up nicely. Obviously he's never known a Tizzard to buy a yellow Kia.

'Tizzard is not an uncommon name in Newfoundland,' Mae points out.

'Precisely,' I add.

'She married a Tizzard,' says Teagan.

'Right,' says Jason. 'She married a Tizzard.' Only mildly deterred by our cautions. 'And likely divorced him, but kept the name to fit in.'

'Jason, man, you're getting carried away. You're jumping to conclusions. This is not good.' I try to remain calm.

He's on his phone. Scanning his list of contacts, it looks like. Hits the number, hits speakerphone, and centres the phone in the middle of the table.

'Hello. Jason?'

'Kaleb, is that you?' Kaleb, the fellow we met outside Gertie's house, the carpenter. From Change Islands.

'It's me. Is there any news?'

'The cops aren't saying anything. Not yet. Kaleb, I have a question.'

'Go ahead.'

'Do you know someone by the name of Rose Tizzard?'

Hesitation. 'Was married to Jack Tizzard.'

Jason is smiling. 'She lives on Change Islands?'

'For now.' More hesitation. 'Since Jack died she's been flittin' around all over the place. Lookin' for another man, if you ask me.'

His smile is even wider. 'She's into crafts, is she?'

'Wha?'

'I mean like sewing. She's into sewing stuff?'

'Got me on that one. Want me to ask the wife?'

The wife would be Connie, if I recall correctly.

There's an exchange out of hearing range, then Kaleb is back on the line. 'Connie's got no idea.'

Jason was obviously hoping for more. But he hasn't given up. 'Thanks, Kaleb. Probably see you later. I'm thinking I just might take a dart over to Change Islands later today.'

'Jason, what's going on?'

Exactly. Just what the frig is Jason up to?

'Curious. That's all, Kaleb.'

'You think she might have had something to do with the murder?'

'We'll talk. By the way, how do I get to your house?'

Kaleb's directions end the phone call. Though it's far from the end of Jason's fixation on Ms. Tizzard and Change Islands.

I try to deter him. 'What about your other theories? What about the grocery store scenarios?'

'They can wait. This is important.'

'This could be a game changer,' adds his backup, Teagan.

Jason is on his phone again. 'The ferry is on time. Leaves at ten. You guys in?'

Are we guys in? In what? In for a wild goose chase?

'Jason, man, you're jumping the gun. You're wasting valuable time.'

'We get the four o'clock ferry back to Fogo. Plenty of time to have a chat with Kaleb, then drop in on the missus and see what's up with her. Back on Fogo by four-thirty. You got a better idea?'

The fact is I have no ideas except to permanently divest myself of Jason.

'Today's my day off,' says Teagan, unnecessarily.

And it's the last full day we have planned for Fogo Island. We're scheduled to leave tomorrow and head back to St. John's. Mae has to get back to work. If there's anything that is perfectly clear at this point it's that my time is better spent where the murder took place, not setting myself up to waste six or seven hours on a Sunday checking out some 'missus' in a sweatshirt on Change Islands.

CHANGING WAYS

BEGRUDGINGLY CROSSING THE seven kilometres between Fogo Island and Change Islands, however, is exactly what I'm doing.

'You never know,' says Mae, seated next to me in the passenger lounge of the MV *Veteran*.

Never know what? That Jason and Teagan are not about to lead us to one iota of evidence that will help solve the case? The zealous couple are currently on deck, where ideally the wind will aerate their brains.

In a seat across from us is Nick. 'Along for the ride,' as he said, having heard my emphatic dismissal of the trip several times. 'We'll take your mind off it.'

The 'we' meaning he and Gaffer. Said dog is in the Toyota on the vehicle deck, confined there with a blanket and a few treats.

So why then did I give in to joining the rogue couple on this senseless jaunt?

Mae. Whose logic was 'What if, by an off chance, there is something to it and Jason royally screws up?'

There is that possibility. But, I will add, a bloody unlikely one.

Let's just say I'm here now, resigned to squandering six hours.

Mae reaches over and squeezes my hand. A bit patronizing, but I can do with any part of me being squeezed. I lay my other hand on top of hers. She squeezes harder.

Nick glances up from his iPhone. 'You two are sweet,' he says.

Sweet, Nick? Calculated to crack through the funk.

I eventually smile. The kid has learned to play me like a fiddle. And get away with it.

The windblown couple joins us inside. Our hands disengage.

'Geared up to go? Ready to rock?' says Jason. His chirpiness is an open threat to my new-found affability.

Fortunately we've almost reached the land of enlightenment. An announcement fills the lounge, instructing passengers to return to their vehicles. We are about to dock in Change Islands.

Gaffer looks to be thrilled with the prospect, which undoubtedly has to do with his disgust at having been left alone in the car.

His enthusiasm is far from infectious, but I have reached the level of faking it. 'Now, folks, are we ready to be underwhelmed?' I'm smiling. I'm chirpy.

Mae shakes her head indulgently but says nothing. Nick, on the other hand, pipes up from the back seat. 'Dad, man, get over yourself.'

There now. Filial advice straight from a sixteen-year-old man of the world.

On second thought, I bite my tongue.

The signal from the ramp attendant comes none too soon. Up we go from the bowels of the ferry and out into the sunshine.

The dawn of a new day, so to speak. Yes, I can find pleasure in following behind Jason's pickup as we make our way from the ferry terminal to the community of Change Islands, over twelve kilometres of what I expect will be nondescript road through ubiquitous stands of spruce.

'Look, off to the right,' says Nick when we're only partway there. 'That's it. The Newfoundland Pony Sanctuary.'

Well now, who's up for a break in the monotony?

'These guys are doing all they can to make sure the pony never goes extinct,' adds Nick. 'Great reviews on Tripadvisor.'

Normally music to a tour guide's ears. But as much as we'd all like to get up close and personal with this exceptional breed, this designated-heritage animal and pillar of the outports for centuries, we haven't got the time.

'Jason is in a mad tear. It's all I can do to keep up with him.'

'The pony numbers in the province have plummeted from thirteen thousand in the 1960s to fewer than four hundred today,' Nick quotes to emphasize his disappointment.

'We'll stop on the way back.'

He's hardly satisfied. Fortunately, only a few minutes later the community of Change Islands reveals itself.

Okay, hit me like a tourism ad. Jar me so that I'm left scrunching my eyes and thinking I've just come upon the quintessential Newfoundland outport, one that sends mainlanders into spasms of heavy breathing. Goddamn it, there's a postcard around every corner.

I leave the words to Mae. 'Extraordinary. Amazing. How beautiful is that.'

Even Nick. 'Wicked.'

And from Gaffer a resounding 'Harf! Harf! Harf! Harf!' Four in a row, which he reserves for moments that particularly amaze him.

We have come to the northern end of the largest of three islands, where a bridge crosses Main Tickle to the centre island. It is here the couple hundred Change Islanders have their homes, their fishing stores and stages, along the shorelines and in and around numerous inlets and coves.

Mae, catching a hint of my admiration, informs us that

Change Islands has been dubbed the 'Fishing Stage Capital of the World.' No doubt about it. They're everywhere, generally red ochre in colour, trimmed in white. And in use. Not just for the cameras.

'Fishermen here in the 1700s,' Mae continues, reading from her phone, playing to the tour guide. 'Population peaked at over a thousand.'

Like most Newfoundland outports, Change Islands was struck hard by the shutdown of the northern cod fishery in 1992. I got to say, the people that remained are keeping the place shipshape. With a fish plant still up and running.

'One of three plants in Newfoundland licensed to process sea cucumber,' says Nick, not to be out-googled by Mae.

'Sea cucumber?'

'A delicacy in Asia. Also used in Chinese medicine to treat impotence, constipation, frequent urination, and joint pain.'

'In that case scratch me off the customer list.'

Chuckles all around. I detect a measure of relief. A glimpse of the old Sebastian, they're thinking.

Maybe. We'll see how the next few hours pan out. Nothing is about to deter me from anticipation of huge disappointment. Starting with a visit to the home of Kaleb and Connie, to which Jason's pickup is leading us at the moment. Rather circuitously. Something is off the mark—either Kaleb's instructions, or Jason's sense of direction. At least every route is the scenic route.

This latest one winds along the shoreline, past the Anglican church and the old Society of United Fishermen hall. Finally Jason hits the brakes. He must recognize Kaleb's pickup at the end the driveway.

It's a long driveway. It brings a sudden, swift jolt, courtesy of the RCMP. There's a cop car parked next to the pickup. The Mounties have preceded us. And here we were thinking we had an open playing field.

The double take dissipates. We knew the cops would want to interview Kaleb at some point.

The cache of Mounties in the detachment on Fogo are also in charge of Change Islands. Efficient lot that they are, they must have dispatched an officer on the early morning ferry. Whoever it is likely showed up at Kaleb's not long after Jason talked to him on the phone. I check the time. Which means they had lots to talk about.

Jason's truck slips by the driveway, eventually stuttering to a stop on the side of the road, well past it. I ease in behind him and park. He exits his vehicle and strolls back.

'We'll have lunch and then come back,' he says through my open window, as if he's got everything under control. 'The cops will be gone by then. I know a good spot.'

'Perfect,' Nick calls from behind me, the teenage appetite overriding any alternate plan. Not that I have one worth suggesting.

Jason's good spot requires a few minutes of backtracking. We repass the cop car, firmly ensconced in the driveway. What's with this drawn-out line of questioning? What do the cops know that we don't?

The PGR Restaurant presents itself in short order. It seems to be following the time-honoured Newfoundland tradition of naming a private enterprise with the initials of the owner's children. In this case it works reasonably well.

'Not so good if you named your kids Amanda, Sophie, and Sam,' quips Nick.

His wit only improving with age, that boy.

The restaurant has a gazebo out front with a charming view of the tickle. The temperature, however, is bit cool for outdoor dining. We'll take the indoor option, and at this point we're the only customers for lunch. A serviceable table for five, and a very welcoming couple, the parents of P, G, and R.

Mandy and Doug are very good at separating the tourists from the near locals. We three are obviously the former. And Jason has only to open his mouth and emit three words.

'How's she goin'?'

They instantly have him pegged as coming from Fogo. Not only does he sound the part, there's something about his facial features that Doug vaguely recognizes.

'You're Jason,' Doug says before long. 'I worked wit' your father.'

And with that Mandy wraps her motherly arms around the young man and hugs him tight, barely holding back her tears. 'Your poor Aunt Gertie. How awful, how awful. My love, nobody can believe it.'

Jason is not surprised by her flourish of affection. No doubt other older women, some perfect strangers, have made similar moves over the past couple of days. He says nothing.

And Teagan they can place as well. Her sister who lives in Twillingate is married to a nephew of someone who lives 'just out the road.'

As for the three of us tourists, we barely escape a connection. They have relatives in St. John's but, disappointingly, no names ring a bell. Mandy does, however, have a fondness for Winners in the Avalon Mall. As does Mae. It's the closest we get.

In due course, our focus is lunch. The twenty-and-under crowd opt for hamburger platters. For Mae and me there's no contest. It has to be the pan-fried cod and home fries. I come to outport Newfoundland and I want nothing resembling burger buns on my plate (unless they have ground moose meat between them).

The cod is brilliant. Hardly out of the water and fried to perfection, each forkful a reason to celebrate this king of the North Atlantic.

We have more than food on our minds, however. Jason is

not long into his burger when he sets it back on his plate and awaits the return of Doug, who has been hovering between the kitchen and the dining area.

'Doug, what can you tell us about Rose Tizzard?'

It catches him off guard and the water jug he's been carrying makes an ungraceful landing on our table.

'Well now.'

It halts our consumption. Not so much as a home fry between the fingers.

'Poor Jack Tizzard's woman?'

Poor as in the deceased Jack Tizzard. 'That's the one.'

'Hardly knows what to be telling you.'

Mandy emerges from the kitchen, having overheard mention of Rose. She lets Doug have his few words as she wipes her hands in her apron.

'Not a friend, is she?' Doug asks. He wants to be sure he's not about to set foot in delicate territory.

'Never met the woman.'

Which clears the way. 'No gettin' around it, she's an odd one. Where she come from we don't know. Jack worked off and on in Ontario for years.'

'Jack never married, my love,' says Mandy, her arms folded. 'Never found the right woman, I suppose. And then about a year before he died he showed up with Rose on his arm. We didn't know what to think, did we, Doug? We figured he must've been someplace foreign.' She's looking as if there had been speculation about a lot more than her place of birth.

'Turned out he met and married her in Sudbury, then drove to Newfoundland. At least that's what he said. A lot of people had their doubts.'

'Knowing Jack, it's just as likely he picked her up hitch-hiking on the 401.'

'Really?' I say to keep the engines going.

'She's not exactly your homebody,' says Mandy. 'Forever on the go.' Then adds in a more disapproving tone, 'Spending Jack's money. Which, I daresay, my love, was more than a few dollars.'

By the sound of it Rose Tizzard doesn't exactly fit into Change Islands.

'Takes all kinds,' says Doug. 'Who are we to judge?'

I sense that's about as charitable an opinion of the woman as we are likely to get.

'She made some friends, did she?' inserts Mae, attempting to stir the pot once more.

'The only one I know of is Connie Cutler.'

'You mean Kaleb's wife?' says Jason.

Mandy nods. 'But I don't know how much of a friend,' she's quick to add. 'They go to Gander shopping, I know that.' She seems to catch herself. 'My love, that's about as much as I can tell you.'

Nobody takes the ferry from Change Islands without somebody knowing. And I'd say where they end up is as clear as the Timbits they snack on during the ferry ride back.

It's back to the cod and fries, somewhat reluctantly I'll admit. I'm sure there's more speculation that, with tourists at the table, we won't be privy to.

I glance at Jason. I know what has now planted itself in his head. Connie Cutler is the new prime informant regarding Rose.

It's still a path to nowhere. Logic has not taken root in that inexperienced mind of his. If Rose Tizzard had anything to do with the murder, why in hell's name would she go about wearing such a blatant sweatshirt? An insensitive sewciopath she might be, a murderer she's not.

The cop car has departed the premises. Replaced by a pair of less noteworthy vehicles. Jason rings the doorbell.

It's a languid Kaleb Cutler who comes to answer it. It doesn't help that it's not only Jason showing up, but three others standing expectantly behind him. I did have the good sense to insist that Nick stay back and walk the dog.

'You don't mind, do you, Kaleb? We're all together.'

In the numerical sense that is. I have no idea how this will play out, given that it's firmly in Jason's impulsive hands.

We parade into a spacious, well-built house, the home of a carpenter after all.

If Kaleb lacks energy, his wife is literally on a couch, with no intention of getting up to greet us. As we pass by the entrance to the living room we can see her stretched out and covered by a quilt. Not even her head is visible.

'Connie's a little under the weather,' explains Kaleb. It may well be that the longish session with the RCMP put her there.

It's a disappointment of course. One of the reasons we're here is to find out what she can tell us about Rose Tizzard. Now it's all in Kaleb's hands. Not quite from the horse's mouth.

Newfoundlanders like a spacious kitchen. This one holds a table large enough to accommodate us all, with room to spare.

We look at each other and smile lightly. There's a need to play it cautiously, with a straightforward but easy touch.

'You're good with a few questions, Kaleb?' Jason says, his voice lower than usual, with Connie in mind.

Well done, Jason. You're learning. Subdued is good.

'I suppose so,' says Kaleb.

'I'll get to the point,' Jason tells him calmly. Then almost under his breath, 'What the hell is going on with Rose Tizzard?'

I cringe. Of course he bulldozes ahead out of control. Of course there was no lead-in to relax the informant. Of course he has zero understanding about building an atmosphere to generate the free flow of conversation. He's Jason. Subdued or not, he hasn't got a bloody clue how to go about doing what he's doing.

Kaleb takes an extended breath. He looks around the table, as if assessing what the reactions might be to what he will say, before returning to the only person he actually knows, the eager young laddio asking the question.

Kaleb, too, is on volume control. 'She's a strange one, Jason. Cracked, if you ask me.'

At times like these you can only shake your head. Unfortunately I can only do so mentally.

For Jason it's an open call to dive deeper. 'Whataya think, Kaleb? She's livin' 'er up offa Jack's money?'

My head shrinks into my shoulders. Why not put words in his mouth? Why not break every bloody interview rule in the book while you're at it?

'She's livin' high on the hog,' says Kaleb, 'no two ways about it.'

'And lovin' every minute of it,' says Jason.

Kaleb chuckles. An odd, sustained chuckle.

Loud enough to bring Connie into the room.

Everyone turns to her. Mae and I glance at each other, eyes wide. I'm figuring she must have been standing just inside the living room. Only far enough away to stay out of sight.

She shows little sign of her session on the couch, except for her slightly disrupted hair. Her outfit is what I would call an exuberant mauve, only somewhat tempered by a longish turquoise cardigan. Something chosen especially for the police visit, I assume.

Kaleb is quick to apologize. 'Sorry we woke you.'

'I wasn't asleep.' Ever so slightly combative.

It's enough to confirm she overheard the conversation. Reconfirmed now by the look she gives Jason.

'Rose is her own woman,' says Connie, quietly but firmly. 'Take her or leave her.'

As if she's said all we need to know.

What response she's expecting from us, I have no idea. Her eyes are now fixed on the one person among the lot of us she knows.

'Jason, I'm sorry about your aunt.' Stiff sympathy. 'I know you'd do anything to find out who's responsible, but you're sadly mistaken if you think Rose had anything to do with it.'

All of a sudden it's Mae who inserts herself. 'You're good friends with her then, Connie?' she says, congenial, yet resolute. The tension jerks up a notch.

Connie looks at her, struggling not to look displeased by the forthrightness of a stranger. 'I know Rose. Well enough to tell you're all wasting your time. I suggest you get Change Islands out of your mind and go back to Fogo.' Even at that she has firmly bitten her tongue.

Her reply is no defence of her friend. If anything, it's an open challenge for us to prove Connie wrong, to pursue Rose with even more vigour than we have already.

Mae is not intimidated. She asks calmly, 'How did Jack Tizzard die?'

A judicious jolt. And where the heck did that come from?

Connie tries to keep herself in check, but then snaps, 'What's that got to do with anything?'

'Was it natural causes?'

'Natural causes? What are you saying? You think Rose is responsible for his death?'

Even Jason didn't make that big a leap.

'Heart attack,' Kaleb inserts, in an attempt to calm the waters. 'He was dead before the ambulance got to the house.'

'No autopsy, I take it?' says Mae.

Connie eyes her. 'No need of one.'

'Good to know,' says Mae. And leaves it at that, easing back in her chair.

It's abundantly clear we've overstayed our welcome.

The withdrawal is awkward. There's no way to slip quietly out the door. The only route takes us single file past a purposely positioned Connie. The mauve dress is even gaudier close-up.

We're finally outside and heading to our vehicles. Jason calls back to Kaleb, who is feeling the need to see us off, 'Take it easy.'

He isn't likely to, not in the immediate future. Connie fills the doorway behind him, ready for his re-entry.

There's one last look back before we drive away. No one to be seen. The door solidly closed.

I turn to Mae. 'Where were you going with that?' I can only mean one thing—her question about Jack Tizzard.

'Testing the limits of Connie's temper. And the limits of her friendship with Rose.'

She's buying into Jason's take on someone he's seen once in an ice cream shop. 'So you think Rose knocked off her husband?'

'No clue. But if you start thinking she killed Gertie, you figure maybe it's not her first time. Actually, I was more interested in Connie's reaction.'

'We got a problem, Mae.' The 'we' is being lenient.

'What's that?'

'Conjecture. It's all conjecture. We've never laid eyes on the woman. We're circling her, talking around her. Building a case against some phantom. Before we go any further we need direct, face-to-face contact.'

'I'm all for that.'

And so am I.

First things first. Nick and Gaffer are nowhere to be seen. I check my phone.

— at museum with sam

What's with that? I read it aloud to Mae, who calls ahead to Teagan, who relays it to Jason.

'Sam's place.' It's Jason, from behind his steering wheel. 'Follow me.'

Sam, I discover five minutes later, is Sam Simms, owner of and guide to the Curiosity Shop Museum.

'It jumped out at me,' says Nick. 'You know, walking along.'

Like father, like son. I'm all about boosting the kid's appetite for history. I see it's paid off nicely. And I see that Gaffer, tight in Nick's arms, has turned into a keener as well.

Sam's place is a one-man operation, from conception to completion, with a lot of collecting in between. The display room is a gold mine of outport history and artifacts.

The ex-history teacher in me applauds his passion. I've seen plenty of outport museums, but few with the character and heart of this one. A lot of it is Sam himself. The man has an enthusiastic story about every item in the place, from biscuit tin to crosscut saw, from World War I rifle to flour-barrel chair.

I notice Jason and Mae nodding to each other. They're both thinking the same thing. Sam must also have anecdotes about his fellow residents, especially one with an interesting history behind her.

'We're looking to drop in on Rose Tizzard,' Jason says to him, after we've finished up a quick tour and added generously to his donation box.

It's obviously caught his attention, but Sam doesn't say anything.

He's reluctant for a reason. Confirming, it seems, that Rose Tizzard's history is more interesting than most. Even so, Sam does nothing more than shrug, smile weakly, and remain tight-lipped.

The others make a move for the door. This is where experience comes into play. There's a pivotal point when outright bluntness is in order.

'I'm a private investigator, Mr. Simms. I work hand in hand with the police.'

(Work with them, yes, just not all the time.)

Mention of the cops is a shock tactic. There's more. 'You've no doubt heard about what happened on Fogo Island. I'm investigating whether Rose Tizzard might have relevant information.'

The trick is to keep it neutral. Start talking murder and potential informants clam up permanently, not wanting to be seen as speculating when the stakes are so high. Yet neither do they want to be seen as playing tough with the police.

What I'm after is that trickle of information he's comfortable releasing, something that touched him directly, that he knows for a fact. And here it comes, I can see it in his eyes.

'Years ago Jack Tizzard donated a few things to the museum. After he died Rose insisted I give one of them back.'

Interesting. 'Do you mind telling me what it was?'

'A sterling silver sewing kit that belonged to his mother.'

Mae's intake of air is controlled but perceptible.

'When was that?' I ask, tone still neutral.

'Probably a month ago now.'

'Would you mind describing it?' says Mae.

He looks unsure. Then he retrieves his phone from a back pocket. 'I took a couple of pictures before she came to collect it. If you want to see them . . .'

'Absolutely,' says Mae. A bit too quick and enthusiastic. She's yet to learn the art of restraint.

Sam searches through his photos until he finds what he's looking for. He turns the screen to Mae. I stand behind her to have a look as Sam scrolls to a second image.

'Beautiful,' Mae says. 'Looks to be a French-made etui.'

What's with the 'etui'?

'I'd say at least a hundred years old. The case and tools—

still in beautiful condition. You must have been so sorry to see it go.'

'Any woman who sewed loved it,' says Sam. 'It was often their favourite item in the whole museum.'

'Would you mind sending me those pictures?'

Nick inserts himself. 'You both have iPhones. You could just AirDrop them.' He shows Sam how to AirDrop the etui.

I'm feeling equally outdated. My skill set also doesn't include the so-called AirDrop. Nick sends me a wink and nod. He likes being one step ahead.

On that note we exit, with one final bit of info—the home of headstrong Rose Tizzard is in the part of Change Islands called Skinner's Harbour.

As it's turned out, the Curiosity Shop Museum has been an unscheduled stop with consequences.

Once outside, we're all into the esoteric etui. Mae's phone gets passed around.

Said item consists of a case made of black lacquered wood with a small silver clasp, opening to an inside lined with blue satin on top and a cushion of darker blue velvet below. Resting on shaped indentations in the velvet are, as Mae points out, the various tools beloved by sewists. Sterling silver and finely embossed, including scissors, thimble, and a receptacle for needles.

In addition to 'An awl, bodkin needle, and stiletto.'

Of course. How uninformed of me not to identify these delicate little gems.

Bringing her cell closer, I zero in on the scissors. Yes, the charming stork, its beak tapered to a fine, dagger-sharp point. I fail to mask my keen attention.

Staring me in the face are varying degrees of self-satisfaction. Yes, folks, there's been a mild surge in my interest in Rose Tizzard. Yes, I'm not above admitting there may be more to her than a wacko sweatshirt.

At least they have the good sense not to be smug. Let's keep it professional, shall we.

I ignore them and focus on the etui. An innocent, much-loved set of sewing tools? Or a tool kit for a murderer?

Jason is all for heading straight to where she lives. He's chomping at the bit.

Descending en masse at her house is far from a good idea. 'One thing we don't want,' I tell them, 'is to overwhelm her, send her into retreat mode and stifle potential conversation.'

'I agree,' says Jason, greenhorn and still very much chomping.

I push my point. 'Experience is paramount here. I'm thinking I should be the one to engage Rose Tizzard, on my own.'

'No way,' he retorts. 'It's me who got us here.'

I was afraid of that. Though not surprised. The young buck is not about to be tethered.

Compromise is in order, unfortunately. 'Are you willing to play it cool and let me take the lead?'

'What odds?' he says.

That handy Newfoundland expression is about as agreeable as he's likely to get.

Skinner's Harbour is not far past the Pentecostal church and the Salvation Army Citadel. We spot the yellow Kia straight away, shutting down any debate about which house it might be. We park at the entrance to her lengthy driveway to allow her the opportunity of seeing the pair of us approach the house.

Before Jason and I are halfway there, Rose Tizzard emerges and stands on the porch, arms folded, waiting for us to reach her. No attention-getting sweatshirt. Rather, a black top and jeans, with an attention-getting trail of flowers embroidered up one leg.

'Connie phoned. She figured you'd show up here. Where's the others?'

A curveball, straight at me. With an accent I can't quite place.

'In the vehicles,' I mutter. I start again. 'We have a dog with us. We didn't want to leave him alone.' Not entirely logical, but there it is.

'I love dogs.' Now she's motioning to the others to come in.

Nothing to do but follow up with a confirming hand gesture of my own. All three and dog exit the vehicles and stroll tentatively up the driveway.

She descends the steps to pet the approaching Gaffer. As the dog licks her hand, she turns to us. 'Come in and let's see what's on your minds. Poor Gertie Pottle. What a disgusting thing to have happen. I can't think how I can be of any help in finding the monster who did it.'

Throws me for a loop. Throws Jason for an even bigger one.

'Just a few questions, Mrs. Tizzard,' I say, a few notches above muttering.

'Please, call me Rose.'

By this time we've all crowded through the door. It's not a big house. We bypass the kitchen in favour of the living room, filling it up.

With introductions comes momentary chit-chat. A chance for me to gain some perspective. Here she is, having spoken to Connie and well aware we have suspicions about her, playing the overly cooperative spectator. Undoubtedly, she's up to something.

My resolve stiffens. Rose Tizzard warrants an iron hand.

'I gather you frequented Quilting in Tilting. You sew, I understand.'

She smiles—involuntarily, I would say. 'I embroider, Mr. Synard.' She stretches her leg, displaying the chain of embroidered flowers. 'I don't quilt.'

I take the leg thrust to be a declaration of innocence. She's determined not to expose the least bit of vulnerability.

'Gertie carried the supplies you needed?'

'Embroiderers need floss. Gertie carried floss.'

Mae spares me. 'Thread.'

Okay. 'And scissors?'

'I have my own.'

'Stork scissors, I take it?'

'That's correct, Mr. Synard.'

I might have struck a nerve.

'Just what are you trying to say?' Overly polite. 'Are you saying that I was the one who pushed the scissors into Gertie Pottle's neck? Please, Mr. Synard.'

Didn't expect that, to be honest. Even so, how did she know the murder weapon? Or even the cause of death? It's not public knowledge. She's faking innocence.

She stands up and exits the room. She returns quickly with a black lacquered box. Opens it and places it in front of me.

Its stork scissors are resting comfortably in their proper place.

'There. I assume that's what you're looking for.'

Not necessarily. There are plenty more stork scissors in the world.

But it's Jason who responds. 'Could I say you're a sewciopath?'

Well-timed and perfectly serious.

Rose doesn't bat an eye. 'Yes, and proud of it.'

Deflection from the obvious matter of what led to the question in the first place.

Has she worn the sweatshirt enough that Jason's question wouldn't have surprised her? I doubt it. And neither does she acknowledge the fact that wearing it in the wake of the murder was more than a bit insensitive.

End of discussion, apparently. She's saying nothing more.

Mae cuts through the chill. 'May I use your washroom?' Her attempt to return a sense of calm to the little heart-to-heart.

'Down the hall to the right,' Rose tells her, back on the overly polite track again. 'You can't miss it.'

Just as Mae leaves the room Gaffer jumps from Nick's arms and onto the living room floor. He approaches Rose, stops, and stares up at her, motionless. He's picked up some negative vibes and pinpointed their location. He's done it in the past with me, when he senses something is not right with the way I'm behaving.

'What's he doing?' Rose says, her tone no longer full of the enthusiasm that was there when she first encountered him. The dog unnerves her. She doesn't know how to react.

I shrug, intentionally nonchalant.

'Please tell him to go away.'

Really, Mrs. Tizzard? A fifteen-pound dog can do that to you? You said you loved dogs. You are without doubt more insecure than you let on.

The mutt has earned his keep. My choice is to exit the house voluntarily before our welcome wears any thinner. That, at least, would make returning a possibility. As Mae reappears I stand up and collect Gaffer in my arms. 'We're off then. Thank you, Rose, for your hospitality.'

I did note she didn't offer tea. When I think about it, nor did Kaleb and Connie. Very un-Newfoundland-like.

As we are about to decamp, Mae, who did not witness the Gaffer episode, has a chipper little observation. 'I love the framed embroidery in your washroom. So intricate. You certainly are accomplished.'

Rose Tizzard smiles, more weakly than would be natural following a compliment. She stands aside as we parade past her and out the door. I'm the last to leave. On the front porch I turn to her standing in the doorway.

'One last question, if you don't mind. Your husband died of a heart attack, we've been told. Is that correct?'

She does mind. 'Yes, Mr. Synard, he did.' She turns away, steps inside, and closes the door behind her. And that's that.

Now for an attempt to make sense of all this. Collectively we have pissed off two women on Change Islands. Either because there is some truth to our suggestion that they know more about the murder of Gertie Pottle than they are willing to disclose, or because they in fact know nothing more and have a damn good right to be pissed off with us for suggesting they do. Either way, we've reached a critical juncture. Where do we take it from here without being accused of harassment?

Besides which we only have a couple of hours before boarding the ferry back to Fogo. We need a place for a private debrief and discussion of where we go from here. 'Preferably over tea and tea buns,' says Mae, only partially in jest. Apparently she, too, was struck by the dearth of hospitality at both houses we visited.

Mae knows of the only prospect for afternoon tea on Change Islands. The Groves Inn. We arrive at the fine-looking establishment we've passed several times. 'I have friends who've stayed here and loved it. A very nice dining room, from what I've been told.'

Of course, we're not checking in, just game for tea and a few buns.

Mae is confident enough to forge ahead and ring the doorbell. I'm just behind her in a supporting role. The others are several paces back, and Gaffer, although he deserves more, is sitting this one out in the car with a few treats.

A smartly dressed older woman answers the door. Amy Groves has been hosting guests at this refurbished fish merchant's mansion for forty years. Our request, however, leaves her somewhat disoriented. Normally, people would have called ahead. And normally, afternoon tea is not something she offers other than to overnight guests.

Mae has the forethought to drop the name of a friend who has stayed at The Groves, several times in fact. Amy remembers her well. As luck would have it, they exchange Christmas cards each year. It's more than enough to settle her mind.

'I only reopened for the season a couple of weeks ago and, fortunately, I haven't been busy as yet.' She's smiling now. Besides, it's not in her nature to turn people away.

Amy and Mae quickly warm to each other. Am I surprised? Soon Mae is helping out in the kitchen, over quilting talk, I assume. The rest of us get as comfortable as we can around a table in the dining room, surrounded by lace curtains, rose-coloured tablecloths, and (as I see when I take a quick look under one of the cups) Royal Albert bone china.

Mae soon arrives with a tray holding an elegant teapot covered in a pattern of yellow roses, together with a crystal sugar bowl and creamer. Amy follows with the companion crystal butter dish and a platter of the same rose design, bearing a carefully arranged stack of raisin tea buns.

I can pull off propriety as needed. And I see Nick is up for the challenge. The lad is into drama at school. I think he sees it as training for a future role.

Amy is aware of Gertie's murder, like everyone else on Change Islands. From Mae she has learned how Jason fits into the picture. She is, of course, filled with compassion.

It washes over him. He's got other things on his mind. 'Is there anything you can tell us about Connie Cutler or Rose Tizzard?'

Amy is perplexed. The young man's question is not a reasonable follow-up to the laying of a platter of tea buns on a finely set table.

Impetuous Jason is not in the least understanding. Amy needs some context here.

'Connie's husband Kaleb was doing some carpentry work for Gertie,' I explain. 'We're just wondering how she took the news.' Which doesn't make complete sense but will have to do.

'And Rose,' says Mae, 'was a regular customer at Quilting in Tilting. We're just wondering, as Sebastian said, how they took the news.'

Thank you, Mae. Amy appears a little less perplexed. She turns back to Jason. 'There's nothing I can tell you, my dear. I live on Change Islands for the few months the inn is open and I don't really know the two women, other than to raise my hand when I drive past them on the road.'

Which is pretty well the automatic response in rural Newfoundland, whether friend or stranger.

'Right,' says Jason. He's not good at disguising his disappointment.

'I do know someone who visited Rose last week,' adds Amy, 'if that's any help.'

Jason revives. 'You mean someone from away?'

'From the States. Her name is Octavia.'

Dumbfounded doesn't do our reactions justice.

'She stayed here for two nights.'

Jason is about to jump back in, but I get ahead of him for fear of what might come out of his mouth. 'That wouldn't happen to be the artist-in-residence on Fogo Island?'

'That's right. Lovely person. So you know her then?'

'Yes,' says Mae. 'What we didn't know is that she's friends with Rose Tizzard.'

'Not exactly friends,' Amy says, a little hesitantly. 'As far as I could tell, they don't really get along.'

I'm not surprised. It would take a particular personality to endure Rose Tizzard.

'Why would she come to see her, then?' Jason fires it in there.

'Exactly.' Reinforcement from Teagan.

Abrupt, but nevertheless the question that's on everyone's mind.

Amy has come to accept Jason for what he is—desperate for answers about his cherished great-aunt. 'She told me she was worried about her, living on her own.'

Worried about her? In which case they must have had some previous connection.

But Amy has nothing more to add to our knowledge of the two women. The rest is all fabric-artist chit-chat. By the time we're through, the plate of tea buns has been demolished, thanks in particular to Jason and Nick. The Royal Albert tea service has held up amazingly well in their inexperienced hands.

Our afternoon respite with Amy at The Groves has left us to reconsider the dynamics of the case. Although we're not done just yet.

Mae escapes into the kitchen with Amy to settle the bill and, when she returns and we're about to leave, Mae leads us into what she calls the library. I don't quite get it.

'Take a seat everyone,' she says. 'I have something to tell you.' She closes the door.

There we sit, amid its bookcases, fireplace, sofa, and array of armchairs. I scan the titles of the well-worn, seemingly antique books in the case closest to me, including *Treasures from Fairy Land* by Greenwood and *Down the Garden Path* by Beverley Nichols. Hopefully not an omen.

Our attention is adrift. What is Mae up to? She looks directly at Jason, who is anxious to be out and about and somehow forging ahead with the investigation. He reluctantly eases back from the edge of the sofa.

'I had an extensive look around the washroom in Rose's house.'

Backtracking is in motion. Okay, so apparently Mae's motive for the washroom trip was not as it appeared. Commendable move on her part. A suspect's washroom can be a hotbed of clues about illicit habits.

'Two things,' says Mae. 'First, the cabinet contained several intense tubes of lipstick by a company called Necromancy Cosmetica.'

Bewilderment follows. Okay, elaboration needed.

Not for Teagan. 'Necromancy,' she says. 'Wow.'

'Maybe not,' Mae says.

The trio of males has definitely been left in the dark.

'You think she was into that?' Teagan asks.

Mae senses our distance from the action. 'Necromancy is conjuring up the dead in order to foretell the future.'

'Fuck' is my muted response. Nick looks over at me.

'Witchcraft, kind of,' says Teagan, genuinely surprised we hadn't heard of it. I had, vaguely.

'Don't jump to conclusions,' Mae says, before my mind bends any farther. 'It's just the name of a cosmetics company. What I think is more important is where the company that makes the lipstick is based.'

'You mean she's not a witch?' says Jason.

'No, but she *does* order lipstick from Puerto Rico.'

'Fuck.' But softer this time.

We all know how Puerto Rico fits into Octavia's picture.

'Secondly,' says Mae. 'I looked through the magazine rack in the washroom. Among them was a book on needlework and embroidery tools.'

I can't wait. A whole section devoted to stork scissors.

'The front page had a name inscribed.'

I'm thinking aloud. 'Her name before she married Jack Tizzard?'

'Just one name,' says Mae. 'Rosalita.'

'Rosalita. You mean Rosalita as in Rose, but Spanish?'

'Puerto Rican Spanish is what I'm thinking.'

'Fuck.' Barely audible but intense.

'That makes three in a row,' says Nick.

I could easily make it four, because now coincidence might just be out the window. I look at Mae. 'Are you thinking . . . that Octavia and Rose . . . Rosalita might be related?'

Her answer is 'Maybe.' But her body language is yes.

'Fuck,' mutters Nick. Testing, testing, like there's an echo in the room.

Stand back and digest the clues. Reconfigure Rose to a Puerto Rican–parented Rosalita who plays a part, somehow, in the life of Puerto Rican–parented Octavia. How close might that relationship be? Cousins? Enough that for whatever reason, they intentionally (on Octavia's part at least) come together. New pieces of the puzzle valiantly making the effort to fit in.

I check my cell. If we're going to make the four o'clock ferry back to Fogo Island, there's no time to spare.

Jason reads my mind. 'There's another run at six-thirty.'

'No point in rushing back,' says Mae. 'We got this far.'

I'm willing to play the devil's advocate. 'Just how far have we gotten?'

'Far enough,' retorts Jason, 'that we go back to Rose . . . or Rosalita . . . or whoever the fuck she is and get some answers.'

I glance at Nick. Unlike my usage of the f-word, his has a vehemence that doesn't serve us well.

'Cool it, Jace.'

A voice of reason. Nice move, Teagan.

'We got far enough,' she adds, 'not to blow it.'

Exactly. 'It's a delicate situation. We're on borderline terms with her to begin with. Even getting past her door might not be easy.'

They're all silent (including the brooding Jason), waiting for my follow-up, presumably a strategy of some sort.

'We'll play it by ear.'

Not big on specifics. It doesn't sit well.

'We can't have her feel she's being attacked, all guns blazing.' My assertiveness appears to be effective. 'And I'll take the lead, of course.'

'Of course,' says Teagan. That girl is a definite asset.

Our return to Skinner's Harbour is underway. More than ever not knowing what to expect.

Like a second vehicle parked in the driveway. A modest white hatchback side by side with the glare-yellow Kia.

For a second I'm thinking it might be better to postpone the encounter until there's only Rosalita in the house. Then again, she's less likely to act up in front of another visitor. Might just tone her down a few notches, show another side of her.

I park just off the road, at the lower end of the driveway, with enough room for Jason to pull in behind me. It will make for a more casual, less intimidating approach. I insist Nick take Gaffer for a walk, to some place further out of harm's way. Both of them resist but I'm adamant.

There's just me strolling up the driveway. And this time no Rose Tizzard standing on the front porch.

I ignore the doorbell and knock. I straighten to my full height. I have no trouble looking calm and collected.

No one comes to the door. But I do hear a voice calling from inside. I try the handle, gently. It's unlocked. I ease the door open to better hear what's being said.

'Get in here!'

Involuntary recoil.

'Do as you're told or someone dies! Shut the door behind you.'

My PI instincts have been hit hard. Stunned but in control.

Of course the next move is crucial. Step into danger or withdraw and perhaps precipitate another murder? If it's not all a con job . . .

It takes nothing to imagine Mae's voice telling me to get the hell out of there.

I step cautiously inside and close the door.

A deep breath and a tentative advance deeper into the house. I get as far as the kitchen. I jerk to a stop. Seated at the table is a wild-eyed Octavia.

And behind her—an equally wild-eyed Rosalita Tizzard. In her hand, hovering inches from Octavia's neck, are scissors. The embossed handles are covered by the tightly closed fist, but the blades of the pointed beak are threateningly visible.

On the table in front of Octavia is a mug of tea, and next to it a side plate of—no doubt about it—Timbits. That elusive show of hospitality resurrected. Someone's had a jaunt into Gander in the last couple of days. Rosalita and her shopping pal Connie? Or maybe, just maybe, Octavia. I hint at a smile.

'If you had any sense, Synard, you'd be on your way back to St. John's by now.'

'Or so you think.' The smile widening past a hint.

'Instead you put the life of this innocent woman on the line.'

It's a con. No way is she about to jab those scissors into the neck of someone related to her.

It's a game, a hoax. With not-so-innocent Octavia a willing partner.

'Put away the scissors, Rose . . . alita.'

If she's surprised I used the name, she covers it well. A good actor, I'll give her that much.

'You, Synard, shut up and pay attention.'

Wouldn't surprise me if she had a background in amateur theatre.

'The three of us are walking out of here and driving away.

You and your sidekicks—you're not going to follow us. You understand?'

'Three?'

Suddenly, out from the living room lumbers Connie Cutler.

I'm stunned, but only momentarily. Reason quickly intervenes.

'I get it. Who thought this up? Octavia, stick to fabric. An actor you're not.'

'You dummy,' says Connie, giving the insult as much punch as it can hold, which is not much.

Connie herself is a lot to take in. The tight jeans and low-cut top add to the scene's sensory overload. Mutton dressed as lamb.

The three of them are in cahoots—the intimidator Rosalita, the fake Octavia, and now the enforcer Connie. One murderer and two henchwomen. Who else is going to pop onto the stage? How about Kaleb? He must have a role to play in all this.

They have one option for getting off Change Islands, and they couldn't just casually hop on the ferry without us cluing into their escape attempt. Instead they faked this scenario to keep us at bay.

The best tactic is to play along. Let them think they have a chance of getting away with it, when of course they haven't got a hope in hell of making it through the wall of cops that will be waiting for them at the ferry terminal in Farewell.

'Hand over your cell,' barks Connie.

Okay. Sure. Keeping in mind there are four others in the vehicles parked outside. Connie grabs the phone.

'Passcode,' she barks. There's no point in arguing.

'Check his contacts,' Rosalita tells her.

'Whataya think I'm doin'?' Connie snaps back. 'Jason. And the nosey one, what's her name?'

'Mae.'

Connie double-thumbs it quickly. 'There,' she says when she finishes. 'That should scare the bejesus out of them. They won't be calling no cops.' She tosses the phone on the table, out of my reach.

Okay. Right. I can handle this.

'Synard, have a Timbit,' says Connie, chuckling. 'It could be your last.'

Add sick sense of humour to the list of Connie's deficiencies.

'I prefer their donuts.'

'Try to make a run for it and that kid of yours is fatherless before you know it.'

This is getting ridiculous. I'll soon have no choice but call their bluff. Let me start by pointing out the obvious.

'You packing a handgun, Connie? A switchblade? Another pair of stork scissors? Don't make me laugh.'

There's a patronizing smile. 'How about this?'

Fingers descend into the depths of her cleavage and, with a careful, exacting manoeuvre, withdraw a sterling silver sewing tool, this one tapered to a needle-sharp point. I recognize its embossed handle, but fail to recall its name, all the while working my head around the fact that the little dagger had been so well cushioned that it did her no physical harm.

'Presto, stiletto!' she declares, with morbid emphasis. As if she's been practising the line for days.

The woman is sadly mistaken if she's thinking she could do me damage with that pitiful excuse for a weapon she's jabbing through the air in my direction. She'd be a heap on the floor before she could figure out what hit her.

Her own phone rings. Checking it produces a half-smile. 'That cockamamie twit got this much right at least.'

Cockamamie twit? It's not only her weapon that needs updating.

She looks up at me. 'Here. Take a look. This is for your benefit.'

I can hardly wait.

It's a picture of Jason, and Teagan clinging to him, on a couch, the barrel of a shotgun pointed at them. What the fuck?

'In case you're wondering, the cockamamie twit would be Kaleb. One hand holding the gun, the other the phone. Unfortunately he couldn't manage a selfie.'

I try to process this.

'Let me speed things up for you. Sweetboy Jason was sucked into visiting our place with a text from his pal Kaleb. Only to find a surprise waiting for him. I assume the gun qualifies as a weapon in your eyes. That's good, because Kaleb will use it unless you crowd stand aside and let us get to the ferry.'

Rosalita jumps in. 'Without any hassle!' Ratcheting up the decibels. 'Try following us and the pair of them will be sporting facefuls of buckshot.' And, failing miserably to sound menacing: 'You got that!'

What I get, you buttheads, is the fact that the jig is up. Your goose is cooked. You're shitbaked and you haven't got a hope in hell of getting away with it.

That's exactly what I get, but for the sake of Jason and Teagan I'll string you along and play your dumbass game until it meets its inevitable end.

I pull a chair back from the table, sit in it, and fold my arms. There's my answer.

Connie moves toward me, waving the stiletto threateningly in the direction of my neck. 'Wouldn't I love to jab you in the carotid.'

Yes, I bet you would. You'd love to but won't. You won't add to the murder tally and up the chances of rotting in the slammer. Just get the hell out of here and let the dead-end scenario play out.

A few more pointless waves of the stiletto and back it goes into its cushy retreat. A useful bit of dexterity for a murderer. If she is, in fact, the one. I wouldn't lay any bets on it at this point. They're all cut from the same cloth.

She checks the time. Yes, Connie, you better get your asses in gear if you're going to make it to the ferry terminal before they crank up the ramp.

Rosalita prods Octavia past me and toward the front door. It's bloody laughable the lengths they're going through to keep up the hoax.

'Drive carefully. Watch out for moose.'

'Don't try to be funny, Synard,' Connie snaps. 'It doesn't become you.'

They're gone, the door shut behind them. They miss my smirk.

I stay put momentarily, long enough for them to board the Kia. I grab my phone from the table—the boneheads forgot to take it—and sprint for the front door. Through its window I see the Kia back onto the grass before driving at normal speed down the driveway and onto the main road. The last thing they want is attention from locals whose text-message gossip would follow them all the way to the ferry terminal.

With the Kia gone from sight, I'm out the door and racing down the driveway. Gaffer comes bounding toward me, Nick and Mae not far behind.

'What's going on?' Mae blurts out.

'A hell of a lot.'

I spew the scene inside the house. It knocks them sideways.

'I told Jason and Teagan not to go,' declares Mae. 'No way would they listen.'

I battle to clear my head. Think it through, Synard. Connie

fires a text to Kaleb from the Kia. She's iron-fisted. Hold the two twits hostage until the ferry's gone.

Or accomplice Kaleb needs out of here as much as they do. Climbs into his truck and races for the ferry to meet up with them?

I'll shoot a text to Jason, hoping it reaches him, hoping like hell the two of them have stayed level-headed through all this.

Just at that moment a truck speeds into the driveway and hits the brakes a few feet away from us. It's raving Jason and frantic Teagan.

And behind him another truck. From it emerges a strung-out but seemingly peaceable Kaleb! Not a cockamamie twit.

Now what the fuck?

'Let's get out of here!' thunders Jason, checking his phone. 'We got exactly ten minutes before they stop loading the ferry!'

Not so goddamn fast. If Jason won't take a few seconds to untangle this shit, Teagan will.

'Kaleb faked holding us hostage so the women would get away without you being butchered.'

Faked? Me butchered? Don't hand me this crap. I glare at Kaleb.

'Connie said she would kill you if I didn't hold them hostage. She had nothing more to lose. One murder was bad enough . . .' He breaks down, sinks under his emotion.

Or it's all bullshit.

Forget the fact I wasn't about to get 'butchered' with a stiletto, and there's still no damn sense to be made of it.

'Why stop faking it now, Kaleb? Why not give the idiots more time to get aboard the ferry before we're on their tails?'

'Gertie is dead because of them. They deserve to be caught.'

'We're running out of time!' Jason injects. 'We're letting them get away.'

As if we're the only goddamn ones to stop them. 'I'm calling the cops. The wharf in Farewell will be jammed with cop cars.'

'Kaleb did that already,' shouts Jason.

'But remember they got that angle covered,' says Kaleb. 'They got Octavia hostage.'

'Bullshit, Kaleb, and you know it.'

'I'm afraid not.'

He's looking serious and I'm trying to figure out what to believe and what the hell not to believe. All the while there's Jason in a jeezly panic.

'I think he's on the level,' Mae says, as calm as she can sound under the circumstances. 'Octavia wouldn't risk her career by involving herself in murder.'

I haul down a deep breath.

As per usual, Mae may be right.

Jason jumps aboard his truck, revs the engine like it's shouting at us to get the hell out of here or he's going without us. Teagan climbs aboard and her door is barely shut before Jason jerks the truck in reverse.

He's gone then, like nobody's damn business but his own, two other vehicles after him, trying to keep up.

WILD GOOSE CHASE

IT'S TWELVE KILOMETRES to the ferry terminal. I'm lurching above the speed limit, trying to keep up with Jason. Impossible.

And, as it turns out—pointless. I get to the loading lane to find a fuming Jason planted between his parked truck and a neon-vested deckhand. The ferry has already boarded its last vehicle. Jason's truck is going nowhere.

I pull to a stop and join the deadlock. Kaleb is not far behind.

'Sorry, my friend,' says the deckhand, who appears ready to walk back aboard the ferry. 'Look at it this way. You're first in line for the seven-thirty.'

'Fuck . . .' says Jason.

'Other than that, you could go as foot passengers.'

'Fuck.'

Profanity will get us nowhere with this guy. I take Jason aside.

'Jason, man, get a grip. We got no other choice. None. Not unless we're willing to kiss the investigation goodbye and leave it all to the cops in Farewell.'

'Yeah, right. No frigging way.' It's an improvement.

'Two minutes,' the deckhand calls over to us. 'Once I'm

aboard, the ramp goes up and we're gone.'

Time flies when you're begrudgingly moving vehicles to a nearby gravel pit. We're in under the wire however, the half-dozen of us, plus bewildered and agitated dog, parading aboard the MV *Veteran*, about to depart for Farewell. Crossing time: twenty-five minutes.

The boss man in the neon vest helps spread the word that all passengers must vacate their vehicles. We're one step ahead on that front. We hoof it up the stairs and into the passenger lounge.

It hits me. No one aboard can escape to their vehicle. For the next twenty-five minutes we're all foot passengers.

We're at the point of no return. Time for the motley team to get our heads in gear and get on with it.

I have one eye scanning for a spot to muster the troops for a summit. The other for sign of the demon trio. They're nowhere to be seen, in the forward Lounge A or its partner in the stern, Lounge B. They're ensconced no doubt on the open deck outside. As far from human eyes as possible, of which there are plenty in the lounges, at the moment all speculating what the roaming herd of us is up to.

Well, shit! Suddenly I'm smacked between the eyes, the scanning stopped dead in its tracks.

Parked at a corner table are Frederick and Samantha.

What the hell? What are they—on their way back to St. John's? That was supposed to be tomorrow.

I'm saved the trouble of asking. Nick is looking into my confounded eyes. 'I texted Frederick, you know, when things started to heat up. Just in case we needed reinforcements.'

'You what?'

Samantha approaches. She wraps her arms around Nick, locking Gaffer between them. He yelps.

That draws immediate attention from a lounge attendant.

'I'm sorry, folks, but pets are not allowed in the lounge. Out of consideration of passengers who might be allergic.'

'No worries there,' I shoot back. 'Our Gaffer is hypoallergenic.'

Not a dent in her expression. 'I'm sorry. That's the regulation. The dog should have remained in your vehicle.'

'We're foot passengers.'

'In that case there's the option of the open deck outside.'

'Bit chilly don't you think? Rain in the forecast.'

'I'm afraid your dog has no choice.'

Sure, put it all on the shoulders of the defenceless animal. Gaffer is insulted, only adding to his anxiety. He yelps louder.

I search for a counter argument. Which would eat up valuable time and likely go nowhere.

So here we are—a cluster of eight humans and dog on the aft deck.

It overlooks the vehicle deck below, its ramp vertical, all vehicles abandoned. I raise a hand to our friend the deckhand. He smiles and gives us a thumbs-up.

If my sense of urgency has waned, it's because it suddenly dawned on me that there's no reason to panic. The situation is well in hand. The renegades are not lounging inside. They are in fact in deck range and have no weapons to take on eight pursuers beyond stork scissors and a stiletto.

It is merely a matter of finding them. And seeing what they'll do when spotted, as they inevitably will be in the next few minutes. Need I add that police officer Olsen, unnecessary reinforcement though he is, does up the level of intimidation about to be directed their way.

Frederick has planted himself among us, so let him plunge in and play his part. Bearing in mind I'm the one with the knowledge of all that's happened so far. I'm firmly in the driver's seat.

'Frederick, my man, good to have you along.' A quick introduction to those who are unaware of who he is. Jason in particular. A stiff, hefty handshake from a cop should simmer him down.

Frederick wants a private chat with me. No problem.

'Sebastian, what the fuck is going on?'

No need to jump the gun, Frederick. 'Keep your cool, man.' I do a quick run-through of what's transpired so far, adding to the adolescent, incomplete version he got from Nick. 'These women are going nowhere, and once they discover who's aboard and on their tails, whatever common sense they have will click in.'

'According to Nick, they have a hostage.'

'According to me, if she is a hostage, which I very much doubt is the case, then do you really think a woman would stab someone in front of eight witnesses when she's already on the hook for murder?'

I could be more emphatic, but restrain myself. No point in poking the bear.

'You're playing a dangerous game, Sebastian.'

A 'game' it is not. 'Dangerous' is overstating it. The cop in him is overriding his ability to reason. 'Between you and me, Frederick, these women are ridiculously far in over their heads. The fact is they have nowhere to go but into the clutches of the RCMP.'

'So the RCMP have been alerted?'

'Yes.'

'You realize nobody from the Fogo detachment can possibly get to Farewell before the next ferry crossing. Gander detachment is an hour away. So is Twillingate. So is Lewisporte.'

Hadn't thought of that, to be honest. In any case, a moot point. 'Sure as hell cop cars racing to Farewell from three detachments can spot a yellow Kia coming toward them.'

I can see it in his bulging eyes. RNC Inspector Olsen thinks I'm very far out of my league. So be it. Narcissism is part of his job description.

The fact remains the RNC has no police jurisdiction in rural Newfoundland. Besides which, the man is on vacation, off duty, and without his mouthpiece, i.e., his side arm. That doesn't stop him of course. He's entitled.

'Tell you what. We'll team up. Go at this together.'

I think I'm being generous. He thinks I'm being condescending. And in the meantime the clock is ticking. I check my phone. 'We have fifteen minutes.'

Being dictated to goes against every grain in his body. Welcome to a new reality, Inspector Olsen.

We rejoin the group. I do a quick survey to see if anything has changed. No sign of the demon trio. Metal stairwells lead to an upper level, and beyond that to a third level. There's a considerable amount of territory to cover.

'If anybody spots one of the women, you are to keep your distance. You're not to engage. Report immediately to myself or Frederick. Understood?'

Olsen's teeth have a serious grip on his tongue. What I'm proposing flies straight in the face of police procedure.

What he still fails to grasp is the full nature of the situation. We're talking three aging women, two of them carrying tools from a sewing kit. Even at that I'm not about to provoke them into doing each other any damage. If it gets to that point, they can reboard the Kia and drive off the ferry and into the clutches of the cops. My strategy is to confront them with the hopelessness of their situation. And then to talk them down. Yes, Frederick, talk them down and save them from what is the truly dangerous game—cops with guns hounding them in a high-speed chase.

And, yes, besides myself and Olsen, the others have a role

to play. I want the three women to see the faces of people impacted by the murder of Gertie, on our terms. Another tactic to bring them to their senses and deter further crime.

It's taking things outside the box for sure. But let's peacefully resolve what is so far a gunless situation. Nobody needs to get hurt. Allow it to reach the point of crossing paths with armed law enforcement, and who knows what might result.

'Understood?' I say again, looking directly at Jason. 'You're not to engage.' He nods. If my observation is correct, Olsen's presence has done the job on him.

I split the troops. Mae, Kaleb, Nick, and dog follow my slow ascent of the stairs to the right. Samantha, Jason, and Teagan trail Olsen up the stairs to the left.

I glance at Olsen and give him a discreet thumbs-up. He mouths something in response. I imagine it to be along the lines of *I can't believe I'm doing this.* Fellow skeptic Samantha, tight at his heels, would appear to be rolling her eyes.

To add to the atmosphere, it has just started to rain. Rain could well play in our favour.

A couple of passengers are leaning against the railing of the next level, curious as to what these slow-moving, circumspect gangs of four are all about. I smile and nod to maintain the necessary façade. And now it appears that the rain is forcing them to take cover. They slip past us and descend the stairs, heading in the direction of the lounge. Nice.

There is no further access beyond this point except up another set of stairs to the one remaining deck. I'm thinking that no other passengers, other than the three we are searching for, have been willing to forego the lounges and expose themselves to the elements. All good.

With calculated precision, up we go to the final level. Wherever they have installed themselves, it has to be somewhere near. They would have run out of options.

They are not to be seen, not immediately. Railing circles an area large enough to hold a double row of bench seating. It's entirely vacant of passengers, except for a teenage couple who appear to be using the outside temperature and rain as motivation to wrap themselves in each other. At the sight of us there's a tricky uncoupling. Sorry, folks.

'The poor guy needs to do his business,' Nick says.

I now see he means Gaffer, who is squirming to get out of his arms.

'It's not long before we're ashore.' I look intently at the mutt. 'Gaffer, you can wait a few more minutes.'

In the meantime I'm checking out a short set of stairs on the starboard side. It descends to a walkway and an overhanging orange lifeboat.

'You know Gaffer, when he's gotta go, he's gotta go,' says Nick.

Great. Let the dog's timing take precedent over the exposure of the clandestine crew. Not what we need at this point.

Plus Samantha is adamant that Nick not wander off looking for somewhere that Gaffer will do his business.

'I'll find a spot,' Jason says. 'Give me the poop bag.'

It's the best suggestion I've heard from Jason all day. I hand him Gaffer's leash. Nick hands him the bag.

While the others hang tight, Olsen and I head to the port side. Duplicate set of stairs, duplicate lifeboat. And again nowhere much to hide unless they are able to contort themselves about the machinery that deploys the lifeboat.

Olsen wants a closer look. He does a nimble dash down the stairs ahead of me and along the walkway. Several times he leans over the railing and gates that cordon off the various pieces of equipment.

Nothing detected. Not so much as a footprint. The crew does an excellent job of keeping the enclosure shipshape. They don't want oily residue playing havoc with their evacuation plan.

Just as we're about to retake the stairs and rejoin the others, a loud bark reaches my ears.

It can only be Gaffer. Shit. Where the frig did Jason take him? He knows better than to let the little yapper draw attention to us.

I do a swift manoeuvre to get past Olsen. I'm up the stairs two steps at a time. Jason is just emerging from the opposite set of stairs.

'Jason, man, what's . . .'

'Someone grabbed him!'

'Gaffer?'

'All I saw was a hand snatch him away by the collar. Then this snarly voice—"Get Synard or the mutt is dead meat."'

For a split second I think Jason's demonstrating a truly sick sense of humour, that Gaffer is suddenly going to pop up the stairs behind him. But when I get past the curtain of rain and I'm staring into his eyes, I can see he's scared shitless.

I circle him and race down the stairs he just came up. The walkway takes a turn to the left and, sweet mother of God, there's the three of them facing me dead on. Planted as far along the walkway as they could get before striking a barrier to a restricted area.

They're wearing cheap, reflective plastic ponchos, the kind you pick up from a dollar store and throw in a glove compartment in case you're caught with a flat tire in a downpour. Three in a row, bright yellow, competition for the Kia.

Their hoods are up and God only knows what's going on with their arms inside. Except Connie's gut is out farther than the others and squirming. Gaffer! The bloody sleveen must have the dog wedged against her with one arm, hand clamped around his muzzle.

Her right hand suddenly darts from beneath the poncho and directly at me. Pressed between her thumb and forefinger, as if it were a dagger, is the damn stiletto. Bloody ridiculous if it didn't end in a needle-sharp point.

Octavia, in the middle, is looking like the wrath of God has descended on her. Either she's a better actor than I thought, or she's petrified.

Out from the other end of the trio flies another arm, Rosalita's, its hand wrapped into a tight fist, stork scissors protruding from it. Bloody surreal. I do a double take through the drizzle.

'Synard,' barks Connie, 'you make one move to stop us getting off this boat and the mutt here gets it good.'

The wretch is for real. 'Connie, put that thing away.'

She snatches her hand from view.

'Stop right now. Let the dog go.'

'I'm not kidding, Synard. Your dog is dead meat.'

'This one gets it, too,' barks Rosalita, waving the scissors in Octavia's direction.

Olsen steps ahead of me. He digs outs his wallet and flashes his identity card. 'Inspector Olsen. RNC. Drop your weapons.'

'Good try,' retorts Connie.

'You're under arrest.'

'Yeah, right,' says Rosalita.

That kind of sums it up.

The problem is Olsen doesn't have any backup. No gun. Nothing.

He tries to look intimidating. It doesn't work.

Suddenly Jason decides it's his turn to have a go at them. As if there's a Plan B.

'Listen here, Connie Cutler, you're making a fool of yourself.'

Right. That's sure to be helpful. He's not done yet.

'Kaleb's on our side. You've run out of fucking road.'

I swear she almost laughs. 'The two-faced weasel,' declares Connie.

'Where is the asshole?' says Rosalita. 'Get him here.'

Not what Jason was hoping for. For a second, he's stymied. 'Okay,' he says finally. 'Have it your way.'

Jason looks in our direction. As if he's tried his best, and now he's ready to turn it back over to us.

We're not in any position to negotiate. Plus Kaleb might be the one to knock some common sense into them. Plus it eats up time.

Jason takes it slowly, backtracking, taking the stairs one at a time, as if that in itself were defiance.

'Haul ass, Jace!' yells Connie.

It jerks him up the stairs and he disappears from sight. I hope to God he doesn't get it in his thick head to play the hero and try something stupid.

Olsen and I have no choice but to stand there looking single-minded and immovable, trying to stave off the anxiety that comes from seeing Gaffer squirm about under Connie's poncho. That arm of hers must be steel. Gaffer's energy has floundered. He's surrendered to her vise grip, except for sporadic flicks of his hind legs.

'We're damn well losing patience,' Rosalita announces.

Just shut up, Rosalita. You're going to pay for this and lose every last iota of patience you ever had.

Octavia hasn't moved, her hood framing a stone face streaked with drizzle. A sham, or shell-shocked? It's looking more and more like the latter.

If it is for real, what do they intend to do with her? Dump her once they're off the boat? Hold onto her in the event the cops chase them down?

Kaleb appears at the top of the stairs, Jason behind him.

'There he is,' declares Connie when she catches sight of him, 'the ratfink of the hour.'

Kaleb doesn't flinch. 'The game is up,' he says quietly, deliberately, his monotone at odds with the tension. 'This is not going to work. Someone else is going to get hurt.'

'You couldn't wait another fifteen minutes? You couldn't wait until the ferry left? You ass!'

'We're foot passengers. We won't be chasing you once we dock. Let's leave that to the police.'

'You called the cops?' barks Rosalita.

Kaleb says nothing more. He glances at Olsen, seemingly a signal for the cop among us to take over.

It is not like Olsen to be struggling for a response. There's an eerie interval of calm.

Before the storm. 'The hell with the lot of you!' declares Rosalita. 'No cop will ever get to Farewell before the ferry does.'

She's obviously taken the silent interval to do the calculations.

'And get it in your stupid heads to stop the unloading and the mutt is dead.'

'The charges against you are bad enough,' says Olsen, admirably restrained. 'Let's put an end to this before they get worse.'

From what we've seen of Connie so far, logic is not in play. 'We're walking out of here, we're boarding our vehicle, and you're not going to stop us. Understood?'

What we do understand is that they're holding the aces. No way will we risk Gaffer getting hurt. To say nothing of Octavia.

Still, it is not like a cop to give in so easily. 'You're living in a fool's paradise.'

Not what they expected of him. The two women look at each other and attempt to smile. Then in unison draw clenched fists from under their ponchos.

They wield the stork scissors and stiletto in space, one at each end of a yellow, three-headed monster. A freakish image to etch in our heads. Their answer to Olsen.

Jason suddenly pulls his phone from his back pocket and snaps a picture.

The idiot. My guts cringe. I manage to lock my expression in neutral while anticipating the inevitable.

'Hand it over, you bloody idiot,' barks Rosalita. Exactly.

She rocks the stork scissors threateningly in the air, until Jason is once again done weighing his options.

He steps toward her. She grips the scissors between her teeth and stretches the hand in front of her.

The phone is not in the hand for long. With one quick flick of her wrist it sails through the air. Up and over the railing and into the perishing North Atlantic.

'So much for the evidence,' says Rosalita, smiling broadly, confirming they're even more in control.

And even further removed from reality. Off their heads and impulsive. And damn it all, dangerous. Olsen and I glance at each other.

They haven't a prayer of getting away with this, yet we've no choice but to give them a wide berth. And enough rope to hang themselves.

We're in a holding pattern. It doesn't last long.

The ferry's PA system kicks in. 'The MV *Veteran* will be docking in Farewell shortly. At this time all passengers are asked to return to their vehicles. Please wait for a signal from our disembarkation crew before starting your engines. Thank you for using the MV *Veteran* and have a safe trip to your destination, wherever that might be.'

Yes, wherever. I know the final destination for at least two of them. Just what will transpire in between is an open question.

The three yellow waddlers walk past us in single file. Then up the stairs and past Nick, his mother, and Mae, leaving them wide-eyed and, now together with us, collectively flummoxed. We trail the trio down to the lounge level, where they conspicuously join the throng of passengers returning to their vehicles. Olsen and I follow them while the others head to where they'll walk off the ferry.

On the vehicle deck we watch the yellow lot weave through the lanes of cars and trucks until they reach the yellow Kia. The colour coordination boggles the mind.

We stand to one side and watch them board their vehicle. Awkwardly, but we are the only ones paying them any attention. Octavia opens a back door and struggles to get inside. Rosalita jostles her into the seat, then whips around to the opposite door and crowds in next to her. That leaves Connie, with Gaffer locked beneath her poncho. I detect some squirming but apparently nothing that the goon can't deal with. She works the driver's seat as far from the steering wheel as it will go, then enters butt first. She closes the door. The goon will be driving one-handed.

The ferry manoeuvres into position to make contact with the dock in Farewell. I spot the same neon-vested deckhand, his arms in directive mode. He is in his element again.

The ramp descends in agonizing increments. Have the cops miraculously made it in time?

The answer is no. No flashing red lights. No armed Mounties ready to pounce. The only vehicles to be seen are the ones lined up to drive on the ferry once those aboard disembark.

Olsen can't delay it any longer. He, too, has got to board his car if he's not to screw up the disembarkation. 'I told Samantha to walk off with the others. I'm tailing the Kia. They won't get far before they hit a roadblock.'

'You're not going without me. No bloody way.'

'You've done your bit, Sebastian. We'll take it from here.'

'Like hell.'

Olsen heads for his vehicle. I'm tight behind him.

He jumps in the driver's seat just as he gets the signal to start the engine. I grab the passenger seat. He's not saying anything. Controlled fuming.

The separate lanes are being channelled into one exit lane. We can see the Kia hit the lip of the ramp and cross it slowly. We're three vehicles behind it. Connie must realize Olsen has a car and that it's behind hers, since she would have seen him had it been ahead.

We're on the ramp and off again, with two pickups between us and the Kia. We're seconds past the lineup of vehicles waiting to board when Olsen is forced to hit the brakes. The pickups have come to a dead stop on the access road that morphs into the highway. Within a few seconds we can see a streak of yellow hit the highway and curve out of sight.

What the hell now? The two drivers ahead are out of their trucks and walking up the road.

'What the hell's going on?' demands Olsen, our frustration in sync.

I open the passenger door. 'Remember—you're going nowhere without me.'

'Just go. We're wasting fucking time.' His cop genes are straining to lock in place.

I leave the passenger door wide open, then rush past the pickups.

'Did you see that!' one of the drivers yells just as I reach them.

In his arms is Gaffer.

'The car stops,' he says, 'and the driver's door swings open, and out flies this dog. The door slams shut, the car takes off like a bat out of hell!'

Gaffer sees me. He barks and squirms until the guy can't hold him any longer. He tears in my direction, practically jumping into my arms. 'Gaffer, Gaffer!' I wrap my arms around him.

'He's your dog?'

'Yes, yes.' They want more of an explanation. 'This woman tried to steal him. Obviously he was more than she could handle.' That's as much as they're going to get.

I start walking back. In near distance, having walked off the ferry, is a striding gang of six, bewildered and about to demand answers.

There's no time. The pair of pickups is driving off. Olsen is blowing his horn at me. I drop Gaffer to the ground and see him race toward Nick, who's at the head of the pack.

'I'll text!' I jump aboard the car and slam the door shut. Olsen smacks it to the gas.

Unfortunately, it's not a cop car Olsen is driving. It's Samantha's aging Subaru.

The Subaru's response is indifference, at best. No way is it about to accelerate in the way a cop has been conditioned to expect.

Obviously Samantha is still not good at preventative maintenance. Regular tune-ups were never on her radar.

'Fuck.' The cop is not a happy camper. The Kia is well away and it's likely to stay like that.

'The roadblock will nail them,' I say. It's little consolation. He's used to being in the dead centre of the action.

I'm texting Mae. I figure she's the most level-headed of the lot.

—*Hold tight. Have a coffee. We'll be back asap. We're following the Kia until it hits the roadblock. Thank God Gaffer is safe. See you soon.*

You'd think she might take a deep breath and consider our priorities.

—*What the hell!* hits my screen in seconds.

Followed, a short time later, by a barrage of texts from various other resentful individuals.

—*Gaffer is still in shock*

—*Jason is pissed you didn't wait for him*

—*There's no damn coffee shop!*

—*This sucks!*

A pause. And one final one.

— *tell Frederick don't forget fuel gauge is broken, stuck on full*

Nice, Samantha. So you didn't fill the tank in Fogo, by the sound of it. Complicate matters, why don't you.

The boyfriend's mind is very far from estimating how much gas is left in the tank. I decide to leave it that way. He's having a hard enough time coping with the fact that one vehicle after another pulls out and passes us.

An abrupt check with Google Maps. Yes, there are gas stations. But with more than a few kilometres to kill before we get to one. With any luck we'll hit the roadblock first.

In the meantime, Olsen is digging out his phone. 'Here, call the RCMP detachment in Gander.' He's not one to break the law by driving with one hand and thumbing his phone with the other. 'The number is in my contacts.'

His iPhone is several models up from mine. Courtesy of his job no doubt.

'Good day. You've reached the Gander detachment of the RCMP. *Bonjour. Vous avez rejoint le détachement de Gander de la GRC.* Please listen to the following options. *Veuillez écouter les options suivantes.*

'For fuck's sake.' It's Olsen, not me.

'If your call is urgent, please press 1. *Si votre appel . . .*'

I jab the keyboard and switch to speaker phone.

An actual person responds. 'Good day. *Bonjour.*'

'This is Inspector Olsen of the RNC, St. John's. I need an

update on the situation with the yellow Kia that just disembarked the Fogo Island ferry. Connect me with your commanding officer. And yes, this is urgent.'

There is a pause while he relays the message, with one hand over the receiver without doubt.

'Staff Sergeant Lennox here. Inspector Olsen, how may I help you?'

Olsen barrels through it, connecting it to the murder investigation.

'I'm afraid we have no knowledge of any such vehicle coming off the ferry.'

'What the fuck . . .' That's me, under my breath.

'Nobody contacted you?' snaps Olsen.

I forcefully inject his name, 'Kaleb Cutler.'

'I'm afraid not.'

'What about the Twillingate detachment? Lewisporte? Carmanville?'

'I would have heard. I'm in constant contact with them. And with the investigative team on the ground in Fogo.'

'Fuck,' we mutter in unison.

What follows is Olsen's rapid-fire explanation. It takes more valuable time, but it spurs the Gander cops into action and, I assume, ricochets to the three other detachments.

How fast can they get on the road and head this way is the first question. When and where will they put up roadblocks are the second and third. I'm deep into Google Maps.

'We should hit the intersection in another ten kilometres. Let's assume the Kia makes it there before a roadblock. The women will have three choices to get to the Trans-Canada—connect to the 330, seventy K direct to Gander. Or the 340, about the same, past Lewisporte to Notre Dame Junction. Or connect to the 320 to Gambo, triple the K. What's your bet?'

'If they got it in their thick heads that the Mounties still don't know, then they're not thinking roadblocks, they're thinking hit the Trans-Canada as fast as they can.'

Maybe they're thinking that, maybe not. 'If the Mounties get their shit together, all three routes will be blocked any time now.'

Not how Olsen would put it, but he agrees. Our decision, however, is still up in the air. Which route do we take? Which route do we bet they'll take?

Whichever it is, we need gas. According to Google Maps there's a gas station due to make an appearance in a few more kilometres. I turn to Olsen. 'Samantha sent this text. I think I better read it to you . . .'

A short time later we stop. He curses while I fill the tank. More time lost.

Another five kilometres to the intersection. Decision crunch time. Right turn to Notre Dame Junction, left turn to Gander and Gambo?

I leave it up to Olsen. He's driving. He's the cop. He screws up, he can't blame me.

Left turn it is. And straight for Gander in the plodding Subaru.

In the meantime—'What the hell is going on with Kaleb? The bugger lied.'

I punch in Mae's number.

Her opening line: 'Sebastian, we're huddled together, freezing.'

No point going there. 'Mae, this is important. Is Kaleb within hearing range?'

'Hearing range? He went off somewhere and hasn't come back.'

'He just took off? Where?'

'Where? If we knew where I'd be telling you.'

'Fuck.'

'Is that the limit of your empathy? The only place warm here is a washroom. You can't expect us to hang out in a wash-room? It stinks.'

'I better go. We're about to hit a roadblock. We figure the cops have intercepted the Kia.'

'Meanwhile, we get hypothermia.'

It's best if I depart, even if it is gracelessly. 'As soon as the cops nab them I'm on my way back. Promise. Gotta go.' I'm not really hanging up on her, even though she might misinterpret it that way.

'Kaleb took off?' says Olsen. Like me, trying to figure what the frig the bugger's up to.

'Could be there was someone waiting to pick him up.'

'Or he had access to a car left on the lot,' he adds quickly.

A definite con job. 'Fuck.'

'He sucked you into thinking he was on your side. Now he's off like a bat out of hell.' No need to remind ourselves of all the vehicles that have passed us since we hit the highway.

It's not adding up. 'If Kaleb wasn't faking it when he had his shotgun aimed at Jason and Teagan, how come, after he let them go, he didn't grab his own pickup right away and take off for the ferry?'

'He was killing time. Making sure you wouldn't get to the ferry before they stopped loading vehicles. But still in time to walk on as foot passengers. And making sure you didn't call the police.'

Tight manoeuvre but the lucky son-of-a-bitch pulled it off.

'I'd say he was figuring there was even the chance you wouldn't board at all, that it would only be him. In which case he'd join up with the women.'

'And once they got to Farewell, they'd ditch the Kia and take off in whatever vehicle Kaleb had waiting for him.'

Needless to say, it didn't work out that way.

'We've no idea what Kaleb's driving. And if does hit a road-block, there's no reason for the Mounties to stop him. He's not in a bloody yellow Kia.'

'But the women are . . .'

I'll admit, it hits Olsen before it hits me.

'Unless,' says Olsen, gentler that I might have expected. 'Unless they pulled off somewhere before they ever got to any roadblock, ditched the Kia, jumped aboard with Kaleb . . .'

'And ditched Octavia in the process.'

'Possibly.'

A picture fills my mind. Of a uselessly yellow Kia vacant on some out-of-sight side road, vacant except for a bound and gagged Octavia. Hopefully still alive.

He hands me his cell. 'Call Gander again.'

'The staff sergeant will be on the road.'

'I don't have his cell number.' And again, louder, 'Call Gander.'

The bilingual humanoid answers. I nail the 1 key. The bilingual human answers. Female this time. I turn the phone toward Olsen.

'Inspector Olsen, RNC. This is urgent. Get in touch with Staff Sergeant Lennox. Tell him to call this number right away.'

'Are you the same RNC officer who called earlier?'

An impatient 'Yes.'

'May I have the number, please?'

'Isn't it on your call display?'

'Just verifying.'

Verifying, while Olsen seethes.

The wait for the call deepens the frustration.

One minute stretches to five. 'He's dealing with a backup of vehicles,' I tell Olsen. It's no help. Five stretches to ten.

During which time a car and a pickup pass us, both of

which break the speed limit, boosting Olsen's blood pressure even more.

'Call bloody Gander again.'

At which point we crest a hill. My finger stops mid-jab.

In the near distance is a roadblock. Three vehicles are lined up to get through. Including the two that just passed us. The Subaru is slightly faster downhill, but even so, by the time we reach the roadblock, all three have been waved through.

Olsen hauls the Subaru off the road just as he spies the staff sergeant. Olsen is out of the car, the door decisively slammed. I'm right behind him.

It is not a reassuring scene. No, no damned Kia stopped. Of any colour. No other vehicle with older man, plus two to three women.

'You had a good look in the back seats?' I interject. I thought it a reasonable question.

They both ignore it. I'll admit it'd be hard for the two women to sink completely out of sight, even if by then they had ditched the yellow ponchos.

Two facts are quickly and painfully clear. The buggers took one of the two other routes. And they're now well on their way to somewhere.

Either west to Port aux Basques and the ferry to mainland Canada, to its other nine provinces and six thousand more kilometres. Or east, most likely to St. John's, in an attempt to escape into the fabric of the city.

There'll be a province-wide alert with descriptions. The cops in Port aux Basques will screen passengers taking the ferry. There'll be cops assigned to airports. Unless they're idiots, the demon lot have routed themselves into St. John's, a city with several access points, where it would be a hopeless, impossible task to set up roadblocks for them all, especially with the mountain of traffic heading home from the May 24th weekend.

'So, what do you think?' I say to Olsen, after we've been back in the Subaru for five minutes, returning to Farewell.

He's not really thinking. He's going ballistic. Contained ballistic, but still, I'd best tread lightly. Cops especially don't cope well with being outsmarted.

'In St. John's they got me to deal with,' he says. 'Let's see how the hell they handle that.'

'Exactly. And me. Let's see how the hell they handle that.'

PICKING UP THE PIECES

ONE STEP AT a time.

For me that means resuscitating the relationship with Mae. The good news is the ferry, having docked not long after we arrived in Farewell, is about to return to Change Islands and Fogo.

Fortuitous good timing. The lounge is nice and warm.

For Olsen it means picking up Samantha and heading into St. John's. With Nick and Gaffer, no questions asked.

'We'll bring anything you left at our place,' I tell Nick. 'I'd say we'll be back sometime after supper tomorrow.' There's a restrained goodbye, dodging the frosty look Samantha directs my way.

It's reserved for me, though she's noticeably coldish with Frederick. Fortunately, the Subaru's heating system works well. Her ire may have thawed by the time they get to the Trans-Canada.

There's an ever-so-light male bonding moment between Olsen and myself.

'Well, you're all wondering what exactly took us so long.' I'm sharing a lounge table with Mae, Jason, and Teagan, their hands clasped around hot cups of tea. I stretch the story to its colourless conclusion.

'You think Octavia is okay?'

'The RCMP are checking all the side roads between Farewell and where they set up roadblocks. It'll take a while.'

Actually not that long. We're fifteen minutes out of Farewell and I get a text from Olsen.

– *Came upon the RCMP just before intersection. Octavia found. Traumatized, but stable. Kia impounded.*

– *10-4.* Short and sweet, though likely obsolete.

Not the time to dig for details. They can wait until I get back to St. John's.

'I knew Octavia wasn't in on their scheme,' says Mae. 'The poor woman. And to think that some people suspected her of killing Gertie.'

Not pointing any fingers. This is good.

Jason is still galled that he missed out on the onshore action, such as it was. 'If I had my hands on that sleazeball Connie Cutler, I'd wring her neck.'

I have no doubt he would, though she might not be the murderer.

'Or that scuzzbag Rosalita,' he adds.

That's where I'd lay my bets. Although one thing still baffles me. 'Why did Rosalita show up in that sweatshirt?'

'I've been thinking a lot about that,' says Teagan. 'I have a theory.'

The other two are dubious. Apparently Teagan's been keeping her idea all to herself. Fine-tuning it, I suspect, while outdoors, trying to keep warm.

'Rosalita is no psychopath. She's a schemer. She and Connie had been planning this for weeks. She orders the sweatshirt online. Connie does the dirty work, but Rosalita's the one to divert our attention.'

I stop her right there. 'Why get our attention at all?

Nobody on Change Islands was a suspect until she shows up at Growlers in the sweatshirt.'

'Wrong. Kaleb was working for Gertie the day she was murdered. He had to be on the list of suspects. They knew it was only a matter of time before the cops showed up to question Kaleb.'

'Then why didn't the three of them just take off while they had the chance before the cops get there?'

'That would be a dead giveaway. It would have been as good as pleading guilty.'

'Still doesn't add up. Why lure all of us? I can't see any purpose in that.'

'They weren't counting on all of us. Just Jace and you. They had a plan to pin it on Jace.'

'Me!' declares Jason. No longer merely surprised. Now thunderstruck.

'Because you have a motive.'

'A fucking motive? What fucking motive?'

Teagan is a bit hesitant, but nevertheless presses on. 'Money, Jace. You told me yourself that in her will almost everything was going to you. That includes whatever her real father left her, which was a lot, you said.'

'Just how were they going to pin it on him?' This is where her theory is bound to crash.

'The RCMP were at their house, right? Before we got there, right? What do you think they told the cop?'

'Keep an eye on that Jason if I were you.' I'm being facetious.

'Right. Not only that, check out his truck. Never know what you might find.'

'Evidence, you mean?' says Mae, who appears to be tentatively buying into Teagan's so-called theory.

'Such as,' says Teagan, emboldened now that she senses she

might have an ally. 'Such as bloodstains.'

'Bloodstains!' Jason again.

'That's my theory. Gertie's blood, put there by Rosalita while we were dealing with Connie and Kaleb inside their house.'

'You're off your rocker,' mutters Jason.

I would agree.

'Wait and see,' counters Teagan. 'Wait till we get to the truck and we'll see if I'm not right.'

The wait is not long. The PA sounds, breaking the concentration. We're about to dock in Change Islands. There's just enough time to disembark, grab the vehicles we left there this afternoon, and reboard the ferry for Fogo.

Hardly time to search for evidence.

But Teagan claims she has some, sealed in a barf bag she picked up before she walked off the ferry.

When we reassemble at the same table, she deposits the bag in the centre and sits back. 'Found under the passenger seat. Go ahead, Jace, open it.'

Superhyper Jason promptly does so, then turns the bag upside down.

The 'evidence' falls onto the table.

A piece of floral fabric, patterned with flower blossoms. Blue, mauve, and pink. Except for an incongruous splash of dark red.

I pick it up for closer examination.

'It does appear to be dried blood.'

Teagan is showing the bare trace of a smile.

'Whose blood?' snaps Jason.

'Kaffe Fassett,' says Mae.

What the . . .

'He designs fabrics. It's Kaffe Fassett's Enchanted line. That one's called Enchanted Blue. Gertie was using it in the quilt she was making.'

'See,' says Teagan, eyes on me. 'My theory is not so dumb after all.'

I smile weakly.

'Whose fucking blood?' says Jason.

'Who do you think?' Teagan replies, a tad self-satisfied.

No need to answer the question. And no need to pose the one that follows.

'How much you wanta bet there's not more where that came from?' Teagan rests her case.

Mae is not quite ready to let it rest. 'Then Octavia shows up unexpectedly and screws it up. Rosalita's plan goes off the rails.'

I retake the lead. 'Octavia has suspicions. She confronts Rosalita. Rosalita has no option but to shut her up. Doesn't want to kill a blood relative, and besides she's more use as a hostage.'

'My thoughts exactly,' says Mae.

By the time the ferry reaches Fogo Island, the sequence of what happened over the course of the day has been firmly set in place. We're all, but especially Jason, in desperate need of downtime. And food. The search of Jason's truck can wait until morning.

I put it to them. 'Whataya say, Scoff or Bangbelly?'

Which of the two best restaurants on the island? A tough choice.

And, as it turns out, a moot one.

Once we're aboard our vehicles and the ramp descends, flashing lights purge our empty guts of all expectations.

Jason is on his cell to me right away. 'Cops?'

'A checkpoint.' The only logical conclusion. The exit is taking forever.

'What the hell are they up to?' says Jason. 'The killer is in St. John's by now.'

Obviously the Fogo Island RCMP have other ideas. I suspect Teagan is about to have another boost to her theory.

The vehicles are bumper to bumper. Every time one gets waved through, we advance another increment. At this rate we'll never make it to a restaurant before closing time.

Jason reaches a dead stop. In a couple of minutes Corporal Leblanc is at my open window.

I know the routine. I hand him my driver's licence. He recognizes me. And yes, we're travelling together with the vehicle ahead.

'Remain in your car. We'll get to you shortly.'

By which he means the time it takes to check out the few vehicles behind us and, one by one, wave them on. Each in turn detours around us, disappearing into the waning evening light.

Teagan had the forethought to call Mae and direct her phone toward the driver's open window. She realizes we need to know what's happening. One step ahead again, that girl.

The exchange between Jason and the officer is not going well.

'What's on the go, b'ys?'

'Please step out of the vehicle, Mr. Pottle.'

'You're kidding, right? No open beer in the truck, I guarantee you that.'

'Step out, put your hands in the air, then rest them on the roof of the vehicle.'

'Really? You know me. Jason. I was keeping an eye on Aunt Gertie's house for you. Right?'

'Just step out and do as I ask.'

'You're not bullshitting me?'

Jason, for frig's sake, just get out. The Mountie is in active-duty mode. What you do is not up for debate.

When I cautiously lean out my open window, I see the driver's door of his truck open. With a certain naïve nonchalance, Jason steps out, shuts the door, turns slowly, and deposits his hands on the roof.

'Now, miss, if you would do the same.' From a second Mountie, female this time, on the passenger side. Corporal Juillard, I suspect.

At this point, the call terminates. But Mae and I have a reasonable view of what's taking place. Teagan knows better than to try to talk her way out of it.

The Mounties do a light frisk and direct the pair to step aside, away from the vehicle. I can see Jason hand over his keys. Corporal Leblanc boards the truck. Jason and Teagan are directed to one of the police vehicles, which they enter through the rear doors. An unsmiling Corporal Juillard tells me to follow them to the RCMP detachment.

Which I do dutifully, without hesitation, Jason's truck ahead of us, our vehicles sandwiched between a pair of police cars, lights flashing unnecessarily, but thankfully not accompanied by sirens.

The RCMP detachment is fifteen minutes away. It is now well past nine o'clock. We sit in a line of four chairs placed against the wall of the detachment's narrow public space. Corporal Juillard's gaze from behind the counter is so serious it is hardly recognizable as belonging to the sewist we had first come to know two nights before. She does, however, respond efficiently to our need for glasses of cold water.

Restaurants are calling it a night, and even though food has been replaced as a priority, I'm tempted to advance the possibility of take-out delivery. A longer look at Corporal Juillard and I conclude she might not see the humour. Mae happens to have a small bag of Jolly Ranchers in her tote. Jason is not keen, but the other three of us are looking for any diversion, each taking time to decide from the choice of flavours. I choose green apple.

'Fuck,' mutters Jason, not loud enough to be heard by the sentry.

I can't see the point of trying to placate him. He has good reason to be shitbaked.

A reason which makes itself abundantly clear with the arrival of Staff Sergeant Lambert and the rotund member of the forensic team whom I encountered in this same space the day before.

Nevertheless he did return with what appears to be a pair of plastic evidence bags, together with the barf bag that had previously been in Teagan's possession. He lays all three on the counter. He's not about to reveal what is inside the two unfamiliar bags, but each is sufficiently expanded to suggest that it something substantial.

This is serious business, and Jason's anxiety level is now through the roof. His breathing is noticeably shallower and more frequent. He's made the mistake of swallowing hard. It plays squarely into Lambert's hands.

'I would like to speak to you in my office, Mr. Pottle.'

Jason stands up slowly, resigned to the dreaded fate.

I'm straight to my feet. 'Mr. Pottle wishes to first consult with his lawyer.'

It's news to Jason. I hold up an open hand to him to stop anything that he might say, no matter how innocently.

Staff Sergeant Lambert, however, is eager to press the issue. 'Is that right, Mr. Pottle? And who might your lawyer be? There's none on Fogo Island.'

'Gander,' I respond, 'there are plenty in Gander.'

Lambert debates her next move. She knows full well Jason has the right to remain silent until he speaks to a lawyer. 'Go ahead, make the call.'

'It's late—it's Sunday, his office is definitely closed,' I point out.

'Mr. Synard, the gentleman is quite capable of responding for himself.' The staff sergeant is nothing if not polite.

'I goes along with whatever Sebastian tells you,' Jason says, showing a slight flash of hopefulness.

Lambert, smart officer that she is, is not about to defy section 10 of the Canadian Charter of Rights and Freedoms.

She scans each of us in turn, as if she's looking for a chink in the armour. We respond with a collective nod.

She turns back to Jason. 'You are to remain on the island until such time as you and your lawyer contact this office, which I assume will be as soon as possible. In the meantime, Mr. Pottle, your vehicle is impounded.' The officer assumes she has regained control of the situation.

'Of course. He will remain within the boundaries of the law.' I offer a smile. It is not reciprocated.

We do, however, depart in peace.

Outside, the four of us aboard my car, Jason has his moment of release.

'Dodged that bullet,' he declares. Adding, 'Sebastian, you were fucking spot on.'

It's the best endorsement that I've had in a while. Hardly quotable, but heartening all the same.

Neither Jason nor Teagan is particularly anxious to go home. We all need food, and the sole option seems to be to go back to our place and see what Mae and I can rustle up, given our limited ingredients.

The end result is French toast, minus the maple syrup. Breakfast well after dark. Despite the banality, we run out of eggs before Jason runs out of appetite.

No beer, but there is Scotch, the exceptional Lagavulin.

Jason's naïveté shows its glaring depth. 'Any ginger ale to mix with it?'

I'm firm on this matter. I have my boundaries. Such defilement is not to be tolerated. 'Sorry, pal. It's straight up or nothing.'

I'm hoping for the nothing. I hate seeing single malts wasted on the thankless.

'I'll give it a go,' he says.

His 'go' ends three shots later, two more than mine since I still have to drive them home. I slip away what remains of the bottle, suggesting we call it a night.

Not before discussion of our next move. Clearly, more first-hand information must reach the staff sergeant if the business of a lawyer is to be dispensed with. I've texted Olsen and explained the situation. He'll be in touch with Lambert in the morning.

The other key to Jason's innocence is Octavia. Presumably she's told her story by now, and it will find its way to Lambert. She's likely in a hotel room recovering, under the watchful eye of the Gander RCMP. Mae could try reaching her through her cell, but we both agree it's likely she doesn't have it, that it's been tossed away by the escapees, not to be seen again. Or if it did survive and is in their hands, then we don't want them seeing any text meant for Octavia.

By tomorrow morning the air should have cleared, with the Gander and Fogo Island detachments on the same page and the contents of any evidence and/or barf bag seen as having been planted in Jason's truck. I like to think that, but I'm not sure I'd bet the bank on it. Cops are not good at backtracking, especially when it means admitting they've been led down the garden path.

Plus the fact that I'm anxious to exit Fogo Island and get back to St. John's, to where the main action has shifted. Plus Mae needs to get back to running her shop.

I look around the table. I suppress any temptation to shrug.

Mae's cell rings. A welcome jolt.

Caller ID says 'Albatross Hotel.' There's only one Albatross, and it's been in Gander forever.

'Oh my God, Octavia!' Mae switches to speaker phone and lays her cell on the table.

'I still had the piece of paper with your number.'

'Are you okay?'

'Not really. I will be, I think.' She starts to cry.

Mae picks up the phone and heads to the bedroom, closing the door behind her.

When she returns, ten minutes later, she's wiping her eyes.

'Poor unfortunate woman. Not only did her cousin turn on her, but she put her through hell.'

'Cousin.' As predicted.

'At least she's alive,' says Jason. Jason's empathy has its limits.

'She's anxious to get back to Fogo. Her car is still on Change Islands, but she'll get it later. I told her I'll meet her when the ferry docks.'

Mae looks toward Jason, although Teagan is the one with eyes fixed on her.

'When Octavia got to Rosalita's place this afternoon, there was no one home. She waited in her car and finally Rosalita showed up. I asked Octavia if she noticed anything odd about her. Nothing that she could recall, but she did say Rosalita was carrying a small Ziploc bag with fabric inside. A bag that Octavia didn't see again once they were in the house.'

'Yes!' declares Teagan. 'Bloodstained pieces she didn't use.' Teagan jabs Jason with her elbow. 'Not off my rocker after all.'

'Once they were in the house and Octavia began asking questions, it started to heat up between them, to the point she figures Rosalita must have texted Connie. Connie arrived. And then, not long after, Sebastian shows up. Suddenly they both turn on her and Octavia's their hostage.'

'Perfect,' says Teagan, whose primary concern is validation of her theory.

Anything else Mae is willing to disclose about the phone conversation will have to wait until Teagan and Jason depart the scene.

That takes another hour, until they're finally exiting my car in Tilting. I assure Jason he has nothing to worry about. 'Get a good night's sleep.'

Easier said than done. No truck, no phone, no sleep by the look of it.

Back at the house, Mae is in pyjamas and drinking chamomile tea. I retrieve what's left of the Lagavulin and sit next to her on the couch.

'Octavia had no idea who picked up the other two women, or why they abandoned her for that matter. When I told her it was Kaleb, she said something very interesting.'

Mae takes a drink of her tea. It builds the anticipation.

'Octavia said she thinks she met him once. At Gertie's house. She had gone by the shop and there was a sign saying closed for lunch, which she found odd. Remember the sign in the shop window?'

I do. 'Quilting is our fate! / Open 10–8.'

'Exactly. So Octavia went to Gertie's house, expecting to find her there. There was a truck parked in the driveway.'

'Kaleb's.'

'Octavia didn't know who it belonged to. Anyway, she rang the doorbell and waited. And waited. Finally a man answered. He told her Gertie was not at home, and that he didn't know where she was. Told her he was renovating the kitchen. But that's it. Never did tell her his name.'

'Could be Gertie went somewhere else for lunch. Maybe a friend's house.'

'Could be. Could be she was inside and Kaleb lied.'

I sense another theory taking shape. 'Continue.'

'Could be he was more than her carpenter.'

That needs a few seconds to process. 'Really? At her age? With Kaleb?'

Mae looks at me. '"If I Were a Carpenter". . .'

Funny how song lyrics pop into a person's head when they're looking for answers to life's question marks. I try to avoid them myself.

'By all accounts Gertie was a lady,' Mae adds.

True enough. Let's get this straight. 'What you're saying is that Connie found out and did Gertie in because of it?'

'Not necessarily.'

'What exactly, then?' I'm waiting.

'Being friends with Rosalita, she discovered they both had reasons to hate Gertie. In Rosalita's case my guess is it had something to do with the inheritance Gertie received from her grandfather.'

'No end to the possibilities.' If I sound dubious, it's because I am.

'Just saying. Trying to cover all the angles. Let's sleep on it.'

Right. Not exactly a reasonable strategy in a criminal investigation.

She sleeps. I lie awake.

Unsatisfied. Again. And in more ways than one, as per usual.

Morning at least brings some clarification. While we're consuming a paltry, eggless breakfast of dry toast and coffee, Olsen calls. Back on home territory, he's sounding upbeat. Eager to activate the web of the RNC.

He's been in touch with Lambert. The staff sergeant has agreed to set the questioning of Jason on hold, 'pending further investigation.'

In the meantime, I connect with Jason, via Teagan. Jason is to stay put on Fogo Island, and his truck remains impounded. He's still not a happy camper, despite the news that the business of a lawyer is now on the back burner.

'Look on the bright side,' I tell him.

He grumbles, 'No phone. No truck to get me to Gander to get a new one. No going to Gander period.'

Right. He might as well have severed his right arm.

I let him know we're heading back to St. John's. 'I'll keep you posted.'

It only intensifies his funk. He hands the phone back to Teagan.

Teagan, on the other hand, is cheered by the prospect of being the go-between. 'Anything we can do from this end, Sebastian, just let us know.'

The thought of Jason's investigative skills let loose on Fogo Island dampens any possibility of taking them up on that offer. 'Thanks. We'll be in touch. Mae sends her best.'

I have the feeling we haven't seen the last of Teagan and Jason. Actually, that wouldn't be so bad. Generation Z of the outports. They've added buzz to our time on Fogo Island, that's for sure.

We pack and load the car in short order. We're sitting idly in the living room, waiting for word from Octavia, taking in the view through the picture windows for a final time. Who would have thought so much could transpire between our first such view on Friday evening and this one Monday morning? A scenic showstopper of a long weekend. If we were to look at it that way.

I draw closer to Mae and slip an arm around her. There's still time.

'I feel we've really connected this weekend.'

She smiles. 'Pandemonium can have unexpected consequences. Actually, I thought I pissed you off quite a few times.'

'Not really.' I don't think she believes me.

'Forgive and forget?'

'Absolutely.'

'You're so subtle.' She chuckles, then nestles her head against my neck.

I feel ignition. Her hand wanders to all the promising places.

Her phone rings, drowning out the libido.

She untangles herself, stands up quickly, and answers the call, silhouetted against the full scenic expanse of the windows. Might have taken my breath away had my breath not been so heavy to begin with.

It's Octavia of course. A quick call. She's just boarded the ferry in Farewell. She looks forward to seeing Mae when it docks in Fogo Island.

As for me, I'm along for more than the ride. Once we're on the road to the ferry terminal, I tell Mae just how much I appreciate the fact she's bonded with Octavia. 'It's definitely given us a leg up in the investigation.'

She smiles, tentatively. She's nervous about meeting Octavia. She's not sure she can be as reassuring to her as she needs to be.

Obviously Octavia is distraught. She needs professional counselling. She's very anxious to get back to Fogo Island.

As it turns out, we are not the only ones who show up at the ferry terminal to meet her. Staff Sergeant Lambert and Corporal Juillard are standing prominently near where the foot passengers exit the ferry.

And with them is Loretta from the Fogo Island Inn. I shouldn't be surprised. As I understand it, the artist residencies were an initiative of Zita Cobb. So of course the welfare of the artists is of prime concern to her.

Loretta acknowledges Mae and me, in a manner not quite so generous as when we last saw her. The staff sergeant may well have added details coloured by her blunt assessment of us.

'Octavia asked us to meet her,' I point out. (Mae specifically, but there's no need to be overly precise.) They need to be well aware we have good reason for being here. I doubt either one of them got the call we did.

As the staff sergeant makes clear, 'The Gander detachment was adamant she be in good hands when she arrived.'

Her assumption being we don't fit the bill. The good hands she's referring to belong to Zita Cobb and her staff. There is no arguing that point.

However, Octavia wants us here. And for obvious reasons. 'We understand her trauma. I saw it first-hand.'

From Loretta's perspective, what Octavia needs is rest and recovery time. A room has been arranged for her at the Inn. A trauma therapist is making her way to Fogo Island as we speak.

A hug from Mae pales in comparison. Nevertheless, we're not about to fade from the scene. I'm determined we'll play our part in whatever scenario unfolds.

Octavia emerges from the ferry, unmistakable in her quilted jacket. Her walk is slow but steady, bearing some degree of confidence.

Mae had only glimpsed the jacket yesterday. She's engrossed by it. Given its bold design, any wear and tear it suffered goes unnoticed—even to me, when I'm focused on the possibility of bloodstains. I detect none.

'Gee's Bend-inspired,' I whisper to her. 'Good use of fat quarters.'

Mae is mute. This is not the time to be complimenting me on my ease with quilting lingo.

Octavia is a few metres away. Her face is expressionless but unfaltering. Any notion of her collapsing into anyone's arms is set aside.

'You're looking well, Octavia, despite your ordeal,' I say before she has quite reached us. I felt the need to be first off the mark. I am, after all, the only one to have had in-person contact with her the day before.

She nods. She's stoic.

'I didn't fear for my life.'

A point, apparently, she needed to make straight away. It strikes me as odd, the wish to defend Rosalita before so much as hello and thank you.

'She held you hostage,' I note as gently as I can. 'I could see how awful it was.'

'Rosie wasn't about to hurt her own cousin.'

Her brisk response tells me she's hanging on to her conclusions with some desperation.

Mae steps between us before I have the chance to say more. The two embrace, hugging each other for several seconds.

True, it is not the time or place to talk about what she experienced. At this point it's enough to confirm she's remained resilient through it all. She needs more time to recover.

This is where Loretta takes over, calmly conversing with Octavia and eventually extending an arm and leading the way to her car.

Staff Sergeant Lambert signs off on behalf of the RCMP, for the time being at least. Until Octavia is sufficiently herself to answer their questions.

Mae and I are left watching the two vehicles drive away. I'm thinking I did rather well, considering the five-to-one female-to-male ratio.

We glance at each other and, without saying anything, make our way to the car.

I don't have to drive far to reach the end of the lineup for vehicles intending to board the MV *Veteran*, to leave Fogo Island behind. Two tenacious townies heading back to their natural habitat.

STACK AND WHACK

MAE IS SURPRISINGLY quiet. Reflecting on all that's happened, I assume. As am I. Reflecting as I drive and thinking ahead to what awaits us in St. John's.

Reflection drops quickly to second place. The next twenty-four hours are crucial to nabbing the fiends.

First question—where have they holed up before making their next move? That next move being to get off Newfoundland and into the anonymous underbelly of mainland Canada. That being a flight out of YYT. It's their most likely option. (Unless they're game to stow away on a container ship.)

To my mind they will have pitched themselves relatively close to the airport. Just how close is debatable.

Once we reach Clarenville and Mae takes over the driving, I run it by her. She's slow to respond. Still reflecting.

'You have to assume the police have issued a press release asking everyone to be on the lookout for three people travelling together.'

I agree. 'Age, height, sex. Rough descriptions.'

'They could book an Airbnb,' she says, 'but that could prove chancy. Regular hotels are out of the question. What

they want is a place where one person checks in, the receptionist asks no questions, and the others access the room directly
from the parking lot without being seen.'

'A sleazy motel, in other words.' Problem is I can't think of
one offhand, not being a person to seek out such places. 'I'm
sure they're out there.'

'It wouldn't have to be right in St. John's.'

'You mean like Mount Pearl.'

'No farther. They'd want quick access to the airport. They'll
buy tickets at the last minute, fly out on separate flights, one at
a time so as not to raise suspicion.'

Apparently she's been doing more than reflecting. I quickly
point out that I also figured they'd buy tickets for separate
flights. I will scrap the idea they checked into one of the two
hotels on the airport access road.

However, there's no scrapping the road completely. For one
simple reason—there lies a Tim Hortons. A prime drawing card
for your average outport inhabitant. Seriously. Tim Hortons
has a profound lure for many rural Newfoundlanders. The
farther away they live from a franchise, the stronger the pull.

'Here's what I think. Ready for this?'

'Go for it,' she says. It might sound like sarcasm, but I'm
sure it's not.

'Kaleb is the driver. He drops Rosalita at the airport. She
marches in to buy her ticket and hopefully get on the flight.
That takes time and Kaleb is not about to drive to the motel
only to drive back to the airport if Rosalita's plan doesn't
work out. Maybe she's on standby, maybe the flight is full. Or
oversold. In any case Kaleb needs a place to hang out until
Rosalita texts to say she's in seat such-and-such, ready for
takeoff. Or she texts bitching about the airlines and needing to
be picked up because she couldn't get a flight. In the meantime,
where does Kaleb go to kill time? There's only one place that'll

do it for him. He caught a glimpse of it as he drove in the access road to the airport.'

'Let me guess.'

'There's no guessing. I'd stake my life on it.'

'Large coffee, double-double. Honey cruller.'

'Possibly apple fritter.'

'Plus a twenty-pack of Timbits to take back to Connie at the motel.'

'Or a forty-pack if he loses all control.'

'Our man Kaleb has no control whatsoever once he's seen that sign. The pressure builds up inside him and the minute Rosalita is through those terminal doors he's outa there, beeline straight for . . . Tim Hortons!'

Mae might be laughing but she undoubtedly knows the scenario has merit. For the remainder of the drive into St. John's we talk about nothing else.

Just how do I stake out what I've now dubbed Tim's–YYT? We weigh the pros and cons of several potential manoeuvres. All involve disguise.

The idea of going undercover rekindles the fire, to say the least. By the time we reach the outskirts of the city, the adrenaline is cresting.

It is, however, the only rekindling of fire in my foreseeable future. Once we reach downtown St. John's, Mae drives straight to her house. She's got a load of office work to catch up on before her store reopens in the morning. She takes a pass on having supper together.

'It's been a wild weekend,' she says outside the car.

Not quite as wild as it could have been. I smile. She leans forward and kisses me with a measure of passion suitable for viewing by passersby.

She needs to get back to her day job, but she's adamant that I keep her posted. 'I'm a phone call away. We'll meet as soon as

I close up shop tomorrow. And Sebastian—be careful.'

'You've been a real trooper through all this. I'll see you tomorrow.'

'Supper at Tim's–YYT?'

'Only if you're in disguise.'

We part chuckling. Keeping a sense of humour is good. She disappears behind her front door.

I'm back to my own devices. To be honest, it's a relief in some ways. I'm basically a take-charge kind of guy. Mae brought a lot to the table over the past couple of days, no two ways about it. But when it comes to the crunch, playing second fiddle doesn't do it for me. I need to be in the driver's seat.

Especially now that the investigation has been restaged on my home turf. I'm primed to jump-start whatever it takes to get those cagey rogues.

When I open my front door on Military Road, the security system doesn't activate. Nick must have preceded me. Both he and his friend Kofi, by the look of the sneakers I sidestep to get to the living room. I expect Gaffer to come bounding from somewhere, but no mutt.

'Hey Nick, what's up?'

Eventually there's feedback from upstairs. 'Hey Dad, I'll be right down.'

When he finally materializes at the bottom of the steps, he's brushing his hair through his fingers and not looking quite up to speed.

'You're back early,' he says. 'You said after supper.'

'Change of plans. Mae has work to do.'

Kofi makes his appearance at this point, descending the stairs, trying to look cool but not quite carrying it off.

'You're probably wondering where Gaffer is,' Nick says. 'I figured I'd check out the place first. You know, turn up the heat. We were just about to go pick him up.'

Which doesn't entirely make sense. My mind detours to what the two of them might have been up to. I stop at that, my forced silence rescuing them from the embarrassment of having to slap together some story.

To be honest I don't really want to know. Better I stay out of it. Nick's old enough and smart enough to be handling it without his father prying into his personal life.

'While you're out I'll pick up some burgers, etcetera.'

'Great!' A bit too enthusiastic.

Maybe not. He knows what I'm talking about when I'm talking etcetera. The mere thought of which causes him to salivate hugely.

The food truck happens to be set up diagonally across the street from my house, in the parking lot of St. Thomas' Church, a location I always find slightly incongruous. Nevertheless their burger combos are wicked. Forget the calorie count. It's so far off the charts that I only resort to it when my defences are down and I'm in need of a quick fix. Besides, I haven't had anything much to eat since the pitiful breakfast.

In a half-hour the two lads show up with Gaffer. Spread out on the kitchen table are a Big McKenna, a Saucy Johnny, and something called the Risk It for the Brisket Burger. Slathered in sauce, and so thick with toppings you have to unlock your jaw to get your mouth around it. Not counting the mounds of Everything Bagel Loaded Fries. And Salt Beef Poutine. Enough said. Guilt is such a useless response.

All else fades into the distance as we attack the food. By the time the boys are ready to depart the house, we're all soundly overloaded.

I'm left alone with my much-inflated stomach, Gaffer, and a dram of Ardbeg. I have found that Scotch is most enjoyable when nothing of note has recently crossed paths with your taste buds. You want to savour the moment without the inconvenience of gastro reflux. I set the dram aside for the time being.

I call Olsen. He's not in a particularly good mood, but willing to talk, once he's found a place where he won't be overheard.

He cuts to the chase. 'There's been nothing new other than the fact that Kaleb Cutler rented a black Toyota Corolla from Hertz in Gander two days ago.'

The car that was left on the Farewell parking lot and that Kaleb later picked up when he made his getaway. 'I'd say he and his missus drove to Gander in his truck, dropped the Corolla, then took the ferry back to Change Islands.'

'Probably.' Olsen isn't much concerned how it happened. 'Unfortunately,' he says, 'black Corollas are all too common.'

Agreed. 'Common as dogshit.'

Gaffer looks up from where he's stretched out on the couch. I swear it's in disgust at the slight to his species. I give him a conciliatory smile. He settles back, in his own good time.

'The plate number will help.'

'Only if someone runs it.' By which he means some police officer on the road who takes the time to run it through the database.

I detect frustration. RCMP vs. RNC frustration. The two posses need to hitch their horses to the same wagon if they're to get the job done.

The Olsen I know is not one to slouch about while the wheels of bureaucracy eat up valuable time. I would have thought, being in the midst of the action yesterday, he would hold special status in the investigation. Apparently not to his satisfaction.

I'm bold enough to put it out there. 'I take it you and Inspector Bowmore have been in touch?' The RCMP inspector we're both well acquainted with on a professional level. (And, in my case, I have to admit, a personal one. Enough to note that it was fairly recent but brief, and that the emotional fallout has almost entirely dissipated.)

'We're meeting first thing in the morning.'

'But in the meantime . . .'

'Let's just say I've made a few enquiries of my own.'

'Any luck?'

Of course he's under no obligation to tell me anything. If my instincts are in good working order, however, I'm detecting something of an "us-versus-them" scenario at play here.

'I've called several hotels. None of the names rang any bells.'

I might suggest he try sleazy motels instead. In any case focusing on where they're hiding out is bound to be less productive than figuring out where they go when they do show their faces in public. I hit Olsen with the basics of my Tim's–YYT theory-in-progress.

There's silence. Then, 'It's possible, I suppose.'

He might at least have made some effort to hide his cynicism. I won't be elaborating on my game plan.

Purebred townies just don't get it. They have no appreciation of the rural mindset. Olsen just can't fathom the disproportionate lure of the Timbit. I'm not saying every outport inhabitant is so inclined, but my sense is that Kaleb and Connie are at the top end of the scale. And Rose, too, given the plate of the little buggers on her kitchen table.

I leave it at that. I'm more than willing to fly solo. Let me be the one to plan and execute. Olsen will be only too sorry for that myopic, pessimistic display.

'We'll keep in touch.'

That we will, when I feel there's a need. I shouldn't be surprised at how Olsen has changed now that he's back on the payroll. It's only a uniform, man. There's no need to close your mind to any idea that doesn't originate within the confines of the RNC.

'I better go,' he says.

'Say hello to Samantha for me.' Sarcasm has its place.

'Good luck. I hope it works out for you.'

'I'm betting dollars to donuts.' End of conversation. Click. It's back to the Ardbeg.

Okay, so all my eggs are in the one basket. A risky line of attack. No fallback position.

Still, I hold firm. Doggedly. Having caught Gaffer's eye, I know I have at least one ardent supporter.

He is particularly keen to witness the physical transformation that gradually takes place. From Sebastian Synard—clean-cut, distinctly cool for fiftyish—to Joe Blow—aging noticeably, confused sense of style, but not yet fading into the woodwork.

I start with the hair. The loose, carefree spike has got to go. Repositioned, with the help of Vaseline, to a flattened comb-back. Firmly in place without looking greasy. It takes a few tries to perfect, but already I'm liking that severe quality, accented with a streak of talcum powder grey.

The face, of course, is the major focus. With the time constraint a beard is out of the question. Thin stubble will have to do, colour enhanced with coffee. Yes, it's amazing what you discover when you google "how to darken facial hair." A paste of Folgers Intensely Dark works wonders.

Severe hair. Sooty stubble. Plus sunglasses. All good. Except the skin tone is a bit too much on the pasty side. Deep in the back of a bathroom cabinet lies a long-out-of-date tube of Clinique for Men Face Bronzer. Yes, I've gone beyond that period in my life. But in this case, thankfully, the evidence remains. No questions asked.

The face is pretty much complete except for a coffee-paste touch-up on the eyebrows. And now for the clothes. The trick is to look needy but not desperate. You want to fit in with the Tim Hortons decor without drawing unwanted attention when you're waiting in line to order a dark roast plus a chocolate glazed.

Luckily I haven't been one to discard clothing until well past its best-before date. How about baggy burgundy sweatpants with a white drawstring? To match the burgundy Converse high-tops with the white laces.

As for the other wardrobe elements, I need to dress in layers. The weather could easily lapse to the winter side of spring. I'm thinking green Beaver Canoe sweatshirt and turquoise Lacoste windbreaker.

All a bit much on the eyes perhaps. Don't want to be drawing second looks. Maybe forget the alligator and opt for the all-pervasive Nike swoosh. More royal blue, less turquoise. You couldn't help but be a colourful dresser in those days.

I give myself the once-over in the full-length mirror. I'm liking it. Makes me look older and outdated, yet kinda retro with-it. 'Whataya think, Gaffer?'

He turns his head, perplexed, then barks loudly. By God, he doesn't recognize his master. He barks again, louder, then chomps into the sweatpants where they bulge around the ankles. The master he knows wouldn't be caught dead in such an outfit.

If I can fool a dog as smart as Gaffer then I'm in very good shape.

I have a great deal riding on Tim's–YYT. I could end up looking like an ill-clad fool in a permanent holding pattern. Or I could just set eyes on one or more of the deadly trio standing in line, so thirsting for coffee and ravenous for a donut and/or Timbit that they pay no attention whatsoever to who might have them square in his sightlines.

I choose the latter scenario.

The drive next morning from my house to the airport access road takes ten minutes. That's one of the beauties of living in St. John's. No matter where you put down stakes, you're not far from the airport. And now that it has installed super-duper hi-tech equipment that allows pilots to see through fog, flights are no longer cancelled for days on end.

Which means that Tim's–YYT has a steady stream of citizens stopping by for their boost of caffeine and sugar. I shouldn't be cynical. I willingly included myself in that number on more than a few occasions. It would almost be un-Canadian not to.

This outlet is not what you'd call spacious. Limited seating capacity for a clientele that generally opts for the drive-thru. Yet big enough to allow a comfortable viewing distance between myself and the renegade out to kill time while waiting for word from the partner in crime inside the terminal.

I haven't entered into this scenario aimlessly, of course. I've done the required homework. I have a printout of flight departures to Halifax, Montreal, and Toronto, and I've scheduled my Tim's–YYT time accordingly.

So. Here I am. Comfortably seated in a fake-leather chair next to an electric "fireplace," with a view across a small table to an identical, but empty, chair. Though fake, the singular line of quavering flame provides a distraction for the intervals when nobody comes through the front doors. It doesn't pretend to be anything other than hokey, which I consider one of its endearing features.

Before me on the table is an extra large black coffee, together with a Fruit Explosion muffin. I've decided against the chocolate glazed in favour of the muffin, given that it's heftier and not a particular favourite of mine, and therefore eating it in small nibbles stretches out its consumption. I may well be seated here for a long time.

Which, in fact, turns out to be the case. An hour in, two flights departed and the muffin long gone, I'm starting to feel like a fixture. Fortunately, after an initial rush, relatively few tables are occupied and the attendant who occasionally appears to clean the newly vacated ones shows no concern that I seemed so firmly entrenched.

My open laptop appears to be the key. I am looking like one of those people who do their online work in coffee shops. I could be engrossed in a university-course assignment. I could be dropping emails to clients. Who knows, I could be writing a novel.

One hour extends to three in a laggardly fashion. Except for quick reorders of coffee and brisk bathroom breaks, I sit seemingly engrossed in the laptop screen while monitoring the entrances and exits. There are several youngish business types ordering a box of assorted donuts to go with a cardboard tray-load of coffees to which have been added multiple combinations of milk, cream, sugar, and Splenda. There's the intermittent flow of neon-vested workers who don't bother to look over the selection of donuts before ordering, regulars who know exactly what they want in life. There's the occasional spiffy-uniformed airline employee who has popped in before starting a shift at the terminal, and the occasional less spiffy one on the way home.

And finally the uncategorized. Those are of particular interest and take the most concentration. I have to assume the renegade I'm hoping for might also be in disguise. He or she may well have stopped at Value Village, purchased an array of outfits and, after clever application of makeup, felt confident enough to head out in public.

Although several come through the door who warrant extra attention, by body build alone, each in turn is rejected.

Then, in the midst of the noon influx of customers, it happens, if not exactly what I had in mind.

Inspector Ailsa Bowmore walks through the door.

She's not in her RCMP garb, but her nondescript pantsuit would suggest she is on duty. That, together with the fact that as she takes her place in the lineup her eyes shift about the room, stopping momentarily at each occupied table.

At mine they stop longer than one hopes would be necessary. I shift my attention back to the computer screen. When I finally glance her way again, she has quit the queue and is walking toward me.

'How are you, Sebastian?'

My first inclination is to graciously suggest she has made a mistake. I remain silent and smile back at her.

'It's the sunglasses. In St. John's there's barely enough reason to wear them outdoors, let alone in. It was that or your eyes. Also a dead giveaway.'

So she remembers that each of my irises is made up of two colours, green and blue, that appear to shift depending on the light conditions. A distinct medical status known as sectoral heterochromia. (Which, by the way, I just happen to share with Benedict Cumberbatch.)

Ailsa did take the opportunity to be up close and personal with my eyes on a number of occasions. That, however, is well in the past. Our relationship at the moment is entirely professional.

I remove the sunglasses. 'Please, have a seat.' She recedes into the fake-leather chair opposite. 'So you've been talking to Olsen.'

'Correct,' she says.

'I guess there are no secrets in murder investigations.'

'What you've come up with is an interesting theory, to say the least. I didn't dismiss it out of hand.'

That's generous of her. One better than her cohort Olsen.

'Have you seen anyone suspicious?'

'Not as yet.'

'There's still time. Stick with it.'

Which I read as: Stick with it. It keeps you off track and out of our hair.

I smile, indulgently this time.

I return to surveillance. The smile quickly disappears.

During the lapse in my attention the customer lineup has expanded considerably. I zero in on each person in turn, starting with the one now being served. She had been at the end of the line when Ailsa dropped out. Skip the six-footer behind her . . .

Then whammo, right between the eyes!

Connie! As large as life.

Addiction to the Timbit—her downfall!

I quickly lean across the table and whisper, 'Connie Cutler. Third in the lineup.'

Inspector Bowmore snaps a look. 'You're sure?'

'Absolutely. I'd recognize that physique anywhere.'

'We'll take it from here.' The inspector is texting, presumably to another officer standing by in a vehicle outside. Presumably to intercept Connie when she exits.

Ailsa waits until Connie reaches the head of the line, then is out the door to oversee the arrest.

Laptop in backpack, I stand with eyes glued to the counter. Sure enough, there's a box of assorted Timbits being assembled for her. No coffee, just the Timbits. Connie, you're so predictable.

She lays out her cash, pockets the change and turns for the door.

It's not her! Shit, shit, shit! It's *not* Connie bloody Cutler!

But there is a resemblance. A definite resemblance.

I'm straight out the door behind her. And she's straight into the uniformed wall of an RCMP officer.

In the sudden shock and awe, she drops the box she is holding. It breaks open and a pile of assorted Timbits is sent rolling across the parking lot. It is not a pretty sight.

'Look what you made me do!' she shouts at the officer.

'Ms. Cutler, you're under arrest.'

Inspector Bowmore is standing a few feet behind the officer. I raise an open hand to her.

'That's not me!' the woman shouts. 'You're out of your mind!' Not a good thing to be saying to a RCMP officer, even if she's not Connie Cutler.

I stride toward Inspector Bowmore. 'Gotta be her sister.'

'Her sister?'

'I know, I know. But they look exactly alike from behind.'

The arresting officer turns to us, confused. Inspector Bowmore, on the other hand is thoroughly pissed, confirmed by the restrained vehemence in her eyes.

Better to switch attention back to the woman, whoever she is.

But she's gone. Just like that.

Damn. Not far, but far enough that she's reached her car.

I race toward it. A red Honda Civic. She's inside with the engine started.

She nails it straight at me, cutting away just in time for a direct run out the exit.

But not before I catch a glimpse of the person sitting next to her. Well, shit!

'Connie Cutler!' I yell back and into the collective ears of the RCMP. 'In the passenger seat!'

Can they ever be forgiven for standing stiff, rooted to the pavement, Timbits beneath their feet?

'I'm not lying! It's her! Plus they almost killed me!'

They're not responding in the way you would expect of police officers. They're hesitating. They're wasting time!

I tear off to my car. Fire the backpack and sunglasses into the passenger seat, jump behind the wheel. Whip past the derelict cops, out the exit, and onto the roundabout. Nail it along the airport access road, in time to glimpse a red car make a right turn at the intersection, toward Portugal Cove.

Good choice! No stoplights. No heavy traffic.

Bad choice! Two-lane road and me headed up their ass.

I strain past the one vehicle that's between us, a beefy pickup that's never seen such balls on a Toyota. Sorry, pal, mark me as a man on a mission.

Dead aim for the Honda, past lengthy, lacklustre Windsor Lake, the city's water supply. Past the intersection to Old Broad Cove Road. Would have been a fitting choice, but in name only, being too unpredictable a road for speed demon Connie 2, who is out to put some asphalt between her and whoever might have it on the brain to follow her.

Not a chance, Connie 2. Takes more than a red Honda Civic. You were sucked in by that cute ad for the heated seats, now you pay the price.

Besides which you're coming in sight of human habitation. Look, landscaping service, garden centre, country club. The sign says 50 km/h. You better slow down or you'll have more than me up your ying-yang.

The speedster is no more. This is residential Portugal Cove. 40 km/h. There are roadside joggers about. Peaceable senior citizens on the way to Elaine's Convenience. Who knows when a stray cat might dart across the road.

No, Connies 1 and 2, slow down, enjoy the scenery. Look, the Bell Island ferry is just about to dock. You're thinking it looks a lot like the Fogo Island ferry. That's because they're sister ships. The *Veteran* and the *Legionnaire*. Carbon copies, like yourselves.

I keep a sensible distance, enough that Red Rover is always

in sight, but not so close it's obvious to them they're being followed. The PI course manual had a lot to say about just such a tactic. I know how to play the game. I know when to make a move.

As did young Tom Picco. Right here, off Portugal Cove, in 1873 a giant squid wrapped a humungous tentacle around a fisherman's dory, hell-bent on dragging it under, when twelve-year-old Tom Picco grabs a hatchet and hacks it free! (The tour guide in me always kicks in when I drive this road.)

The road suddenly angles up, and my brain snaps back. A swerve to the left, past Holy Rosary Church. Houses are thinning out, Red Rover hits the gas. A relatively straight stretch before veering right. Now Beachy Cove Road.

Up ahead is a small parking lot and the path down to secluded Beachy Cove beach. I know it well.

What I don't know is the flashing red lights just beyond it. Just before the road veers left again and inland. A sweet bloody roadblock!

Inspector Bowmore had second thoughts. And here she comes, her cop car right behind me, right up my ying-yang. And out of the roadblocking vehicle, one Inspector Frederick Olsen. The RCMP and the RNC in perfect sync! Sublime. Yes, a joy to behold.

The Connies have no choice but to hit the brakes and deposit themselves in the parking lot. And then no choice but to stick to the Honda and hope for a miracle. Or make a run for it down the path to the beach and hope for a miracle.

They choose the latter, the more entertaining choice. It does their sisterly self-images no good to be scuttering unarmed down the rock-strewn decline, trying to make it look like they could possibly escape.

They do reach level ground, thanks to the goodwill (and, dare I say, amusement) of the officers trailing them. The women are now faced with three choices, all scenic, but, unfortunately for them, all with the same endgame. To the left is a steep, exhausting set of rustic steps that leads to a coastline trail. In front of them is a narrow pebbly beach graced by the freezing North Atlantic, flanked on both sides by walls of rock. And to the right a marshy path leading to a thunderous waterfall whose torrent drains into the same frigid sea.

Thanks to what remains of their good sense, they stay put.

As they stand glumly side by side, the resemblance is even more striking. I glance at Ailsa to confirm the obvious.

The original does have a slightly more penetrating glare and spiteful scowl. I point a hand toward her. 'May I introduce Connie Cutler.' Her scowl intensifies.

Olsen points to her partner in crime. She reluctantly takes the hint.

'It wasn't me. Constance got me into this.'

'Like ducks I did.'

Now there's a colourful rural Newfoundland expression, enriching the moment even more. One I haven't heard in a very long time.

The officers don't have a sweet clue what she means. 'She says it's all nonsense. Obviously she's in denial.'

Eventually it emerges that we have before us Constance (a.k.a. Connie) Cutler and her twin sister Cornelia (a.k.a. Corrie) Muller.

'Fraternal.'

Ailsa corrects me. 'Sororal.'

Never knew there was such a word. Language is a minefield these days. Leaves me wondering if unintentional political incorrectness played a part in ending the personal relationship I once had with the inspector.

Regardless, the non-identical twins are in serious shit. They are about to face a series of intense, penetrating questions from our man Inspector Olsen at RNC Headquarters and/or from our woman Inspector Bowmore at RCMP Headquarters.

I'm not invited. Nor did I expect to be. Deserted in Beachy Cove and left to my own devices.

Which happen to be considerable. Beginning with Canada 411.

My guess is there aren't many Mullers in St. John's, and even fewer C Mullers.

And indeed I'm right. There's just one. With an address generously attached to the phone number.

I recognize the street name. It's in a neighbourhood of the city known as Georgetown, or Georgestown to the more sober-minded and historically correct. The street is not far from the Georgetown Pub, I do believe.

I pocket my cell and head straight back into St. John's, eventually finding a parking spot in the epicentre of the neighbourhood, meaning my sightlines extend not only to the pub, but also to the Georgestown Bakery and the Georgestown Café and Bookshelf. A parking spot wisely chosen for the fact that, should anything go awry and I end up missing, my car will be swiftly discovered.

The distance between it and the C Muller residence is minimal but enough that I can appear to have come upon the house while walking aimlessly on foot.

I return the sunglasses to their rightful position on my face, my disguise offering even more confidence now that I'm outdoors and in sunshine. Before heading off I do few quick limbering up stretches, using the bumper of the car. Then a little jogging on the spot to further account for my outfit.

I make a quick, casual stop at both the bakery and the café, to further establish my presence in the neighbourhood, again useful were I to vanish. I emerge from one establishment with a croissant, from the other with a double espresso. I walk slowly, casually consuming both, eventually crushing the empty paper cup and bag and depositing them in a pocket of the sweatpants for later recycling.

By which time I have spotted the house from a distance. It's one of the multicoloured townhouses that line the street on both sides and have been standing there for the last hundred years. It's a relatively quiet shade of purple. Its front entrance opens onto the sidewalk in full public view. As a result my primary interest will eventually come to rest at its rear entrance.

Approaching the house, maintaining a steady pace while noting the stained-glass panel in the front door, I begin counting the houses from it to the cross street farther along. There I take a right turn and, as anticipated, not far on is another right turn into a narrow but drivable laneway, along the length of which are the backyards and parking spots for the houses I've just passed. I count in reverse to locate the rear entrance of interest. The back of the house is the same colour as the front (not always the case). There's a small fenced yard between it and the laneway, as well as a parking spot that would have, in a pinch, space enough for two vehicles.

Only half of it is now occupied, by a common-as-dogshit black Toyota Corolla. Awesome. The car has been backed into the lot so its one and only licence plate is not visible to anyone walking by. Good thinking, Kaleb.

But not good enough. Your Hertzmobile is going nowhere, Kaleb my man.

This is where a pocket knife comes in handy. By law a Canadian PI is not permitted to carry firearms, nor is any Canadian citizen permitted to carry a knife that flicks open automatically. But he is permitted to have in his pocket a Norwegian hand-crafted folding knife that, gripped by its handle of polished curly birch, delivers a mere 5.5 cm of triple-laminated stainless

steel and a Scandinavian grind that's pure perfection. Invest-
ment of a lifetime, the small but exquisite Helle Kletten. As
I like to say, one helluva knife.

Perfect for discreetly puncturing both front tires.

The faint, collective hiss is a sigh of relief. Whoever is in the
house will be making no escape, unless foolishly on foot.

Now to the question of who exactly is in the house. And
whether they would be able to scrounge up weapons of some
sort on short notice. This is where common sense clamours
for attention. Do I go it alone, or do I at least inform Olsen of
my whereabouts, as a precaution, in case I knock on the door
and am met with more than I can handle? Do I sacrifice all the
glory for an RNC safety net?

Think of it as a compromise. I compose a text to Olsen.
But to keep my self-esteem at its optimal level I'll hold off
dispatching it. If and when it is needed, all it will take to send
it is a quick flick of the thumb.

I open the gate to a sad attempt at gardening and proceed
in the direction of the back door. I do so with considerable
confidence, with one hand in the pocket, stroking the Helle
Kletten.

A deep breath, followed by a forceful, side-of-the-fist rap
on the door. No point in being half-hearted. We have reached
the hour of reckoning. Show your criminal face and we'll get
on with it!

No one answers. A second rap. No one answers.

Whoever might be inside has no intention of showing up
at the door. And is counting on whoever is outside to give
up and go away.

No such luck. My hand circles the doorknob. I ease in to a
firm grip, then very slowly direct pressure counter-clockwise.

It turns. I'm surprised. Accidentally or deliberately unlocked?

There's no other logical choice except to push forward and

fend off my sudden surge of insecurity. I thrust the door open wide. It bangs against whatever is in its way.

I call out, emphatically, 'Whoever you are, you're going nowhere!'

I step inside. Inch my way forward.

Suddenly a foot springs from a side closet. Impacts the door, slams it shut! The rest of the body springs from inside the nest of hanging coats.

Projecting from her fist is something she wields like a weapon. She hisses and thrusts it toward me!

What the fuck? A pair of pointy pink spikes that look almost like cat ears. Gripped by two fingers poked through holes below them.

'Miss Kitty wants to play.' Good God, the woman is insane.

The fist lunges toward me. I jerk my head back just in time, flinging an open hand in the direction of her face.

The spikes rip across my palm. Fuck! I escape deeper into the house.

Bloodied or not, the hand digs into the pocket and jerks out the knife. Before she gets back within lunging distance the blade is locked in place and aimed straight at her. The cat ears suddenly look pathetic.

I fend the woman off with my right hand, dig out my cell with the left. It means one-handing it with the thumb. Desperation kicks in. Finally I manage to hit 'send'!

Just as some bloody thing whacks me in the back. I crash to the floor.

When I regain my senses I'm seated in a rigid chair, its comfort level not helped by the acute pain along my vertebrae. A throbbing right hand rests in my lap, wrapped in what I take to be a dishtowel. It's so soaked in blood I can't tell.

It's a struggle to stabilize my breathing, especially given

what sits across from me. She flexes her pink, blood-tipped cat's ears with one hand, twitches the open Helle Kletten blade with the other.

'So, Synard, you got a whole lot more than you expected.'

Of course it's Rosalita. The dye job on the hair and reams of makeup weren't about to disguise that spite and vitriol.

Standing to one side is Kaleb, whose disguise is even more pathetic. You were already balding, Kaleb. Shaving off what was left on your head was outright dumb, especially in combination with a fake moustache. Besides, no sweater, no matter how ugly, is about to hide that gut of yours.

To his credit, Kaleb looks entirely shitbaked. He doesn't play the villain well.

'What do we do now?' he says to Rosalita, without any attempt to disguise the desperation in his voice.

'We get out of here, you ass.'

He says nothing. Kaleb appears well along in the process of learning to shut up and do as he's told.

First, though, they need to do something to prevent me from chasing them. The fact that I don't have a knife wound anywhere on my body suggests that Rosalita has decided against adding me to the murder count.

'Get the rope,' she barks.

The rope in question is (no surprise) neon yellow and braided for added strength. Kaleb is well used to handling it, to judge by the adept way he affixes my legs to those of the chair, then winds the rope several times around my chest and the back of the chair, ending with an efficient series of knots that bind my two hands and the bloodied tea towel behind my back. The last manoeuvre hurts like fucking hell.

Rosalita is just about to gag me with another dishtowel when there's a sudden, heavy pounding on the front door. She snaps a glance at Kaleb, who's been neatly coiling the leftover rope.

'Open up! It's the police. Open up!'

The pair snap a look at each other before making a frantic scramble in the direction of the back door.

What I wouldn't give to witness their discovery of the flaccid black Corolla that will get them absolutely nowhere.

The pounding on the front door intensifies. Finally, there's the welcome but sad crash of stained glass and the sound of the door scraping open.

'Quick!' I'm straining to be freed.

The officer has come prepared. He produces a knife of his own and proves a nimble man around the knots. Within seconds he's set me loose.

I stagger out the back door and past the gate.

Flashing red lights hit me in the face.

The passenger door of the cop car springs open. It's Olsen. I've never been goddamn happier to lay eyes on the fellow.

'Fuck, man,' he exclaims. 'What the hell. I hardly recognize you.'

I rest my good hand on his shoulder to keep me upright. 'Did you get them?'

'Look behind you.'

'I remove my hand, which unfortunately has been in close contact with the injured one. It leaves a nasty bloodstain on his uniform.

Behind me is another cop car, lights flashing, creeping forward from the other end of the lane.

Halfway between the team of frantic lights are a man and a woman circling each other. Misfit deer caught in the throbbing glare of high beams.

The cop car in the distance hits its siren, a split-second blare. The pair lurch in our direction. Another quick blare. Another herding lurch.

There'll be no lurch past a cop car. None between the unbroken line of houses on both sides of the lane.

A few metres from us the pair lurch their last.

Despite the hair job, the hideous makeup, the hand bearing cat's ears and knife hanging limply at her side, Rosalita still manages a taunting sneer. As for Kaleb, his quavering hands against a quavering gut signal panic.

'It wasn't me,' he blurts out. 'I didn't kill her.'

'Like hell you didn't!' Rosalita reels toward him. He draws back, his hands open in the air. She flings herself in his direction, the knife targeting his gut.

Officers race from both directions, guns on full display. She's at least smart enough to collapse to the pavement. In two seconds cops are standing over her, guns taking dead aim while handcuffs finally shut her up.

'This guy needs an ambulance,' one of the cops yells.

Any hope they had of escape has been sandwiched between armed officers of not one, but two police forces. Out from the other vehicle steps Inspector Bowmore. If she's sorry I got to the pathetic pair before she did, she's not showing it.

She and Olsen have their jobs to do, their subordinates to direct. I watch as Rosalita is led away. There's no hiding my contempt.

Rosalita returns the look with contempt of her own, a reaction that only hardens my opinion that she's the one who did the deed, who ended Gertie's life so violently, for whatever reason.

Kaleb is removed on a stretcher. The man who chose to wallop me in the back and not the head. He's far from dead, likely saved by a depth of gut fat greater than the 5.5 cm blade of the Helle Kletten. If his look is to be believed, he's the decent outport man caught in a trap of other people's doing. Is he really? Or just working hard at looking the part?

With the two removed from the scene, Inspector Bowmore turns to me. 'Are you okay? You look like you've been through hell.'

I appreciate the sympathy, even if it's sounding somewhat tempered. 'It's the outfit really. I'll be fine.'

'You need to see a doctor about that hand,' Olsen declares. 'And what the hell was going on with your breathing?'

'A frying pan packs a punch.' Which must sound unbelievable to a man more used to dealing in stab wounds and bullet holes. 'I'll be fine.'

'You can't drive to the hospital with your hand in that state.'

'I still have one good one.' I try smiling.

'No need to be a martyr, Sebastian,' Bowmore says.

I take that for what it's worth.

'Look how swollen it is,' she adds. 'One thing you don't want is infection.'

'I'm calling an ambulance,' says Olsen.

Okay, okay. I'll let them have their way.

FULL CIRCLE

ON THE PLUS side, showing up in Emergency in an ambulance means I'm seen by a doctor straightaway, rather than walking in off the street and being exiled to a waiting room for hours.

And now here I am back home, at ease in the comfy chair, Gaffer asleep in his dog bed on the floor to the right of me, a peaty dram on an end table to the left and within reach of my good hand. Nick in the kitchen, whipping up supper, compassionate son that he is.

As for my other hand, it's been expertly disinfected and very nicely stitched and bandaged. Now immobile and healing comfortably inside a splint that extends from the tips of my fingers to just past my wrist. The splint apparatus sports a sky-blue hi-tech fabric and looks very spiffy against the pillow that elevates it to keep the swelling under control.

'It's ready,' Nick yells. The 'it' is his specialty—grilled cheese sandwiches, filled with a fusion of shredded cheeses and crispy bacon, the outsides spread with a butter, mayo, onion, and Parmesan combo before being fried to perfection.

'Amazing.'

'You mean amazing you got off with only cuts on the hand.'

I smile. He knows what I meant. 'I was more careful this time.'

'That's debatable. Why did you even go in that house? The cops would have handled it.'

'There was no time to spare. I had no idea how long it would take them to get there.'

'Not very long as a matter of fact. Plus you had already slashed the tires. Let's face it, Dad, your ego tends to get in the way of your common sense sometimes.'

Really? My sixteen-year-old son now playing psychoanalyst. No comment.

He knows I'm not impressed. 'Just saying. You need to watch your ass, that's all. They might have had a gun. Then you would have been up shit creek.'

Dressing his rebuke in the vernacular is not going to work. 'They had no guns with them and no way would Corrie Muller have owned a gun.'

'Okay, okay. But still . . .'

He stops at that. Wise kid, he knows when to back off.

'You up for dessert?' he says. Not quite calming the waters, but I appreciate the effort.

'Sure.'

He cuts up some fruit, which we fork into chocolate that he's melted in the microwave.

'Awesome.'

'Not bad. Mango and kiwi would have been good.'

That's better. 'Next time.'

All's back on an even keel by the time he's ready to head off, back to his mother's place. I hug him as he goes out the door. I swear he's grown in the last twenty-four hours.

'Say hi to your mom. And Frederick.' You can't say I don't try.

'I will. Love ya, Dad.'

Reading is a breeze now that I've perfected the art of turning pages with one hand. An e-book version would be less demanding, but I prefer the challenge, not to mention the feel, of honest-to-goodness paper.

The dram is a new kid on the block—Ardbeg's Wee Beastie. Only a five-year-old but packing a smoky punch, a wallop to the senses much preferable to the other one I recently received.

The book is *Dead Souls* by Nikolai Gogol. The fetching title stands out as one of the slimmer volumes among a collection of classic Russian novels that, though largely unread, look quite handsome on my bookshelf in their uniform Everyman's Library editions. An esoteric choice for my whisky/book blog, you might say—nineteenth-century absurdist fiction. I read the novel's dust jacket and I felt the urge, as it were, having just come through encounters with Kaleb, Connie, Corrie, and Rosalita, an absurdist foursome if there ever was one.

As criminals, they were so far out of their depth it was almost farcical at times. At other times I came close to pitying them.

Yet a gruesome murder did take place. A much-loved woman lost her life. One of them did it and the other three aided and abetted. There stand the facts as I see them.

Whether it was premeditated or a sudden act of passion has yet to be determined. What I do know is that it was an anomaly. Fogo and Change Islands rarely experience violent crime. Leading me to conclude it was a domestic dispute that got abruptly and horribly out of hand.

Of course where I'd like to have been is in the room when each of them was interrogated. That wasn't going to happen. So I am left to count on the next best thing—an update from a presiding officer, either Inspector Olsen or Inspector Bowmore, or both. I deserve that at least. As does Mae.

Mae, when she shows up after work, is all over me with

questions about what has gone on in her absence. I attempt to downplay the attack on my hand, but there has to be a reason for the splint.

'Don't tell me you did something foolish.'

No, I'm not about to tell her that. 'Ever hear of a weapon that fits over your knuckles and is shaped like a cat?'

'You mean the kitty cat knuckle dusters with the rigid plastic ears? Illegal in Canada.'

Where have I been all these years? Or for that matter, where has Mae been that she knows these things? My eyes widen in anticipation.

'Sometimes it's late when I close up the shop. Walking alone through the parking lot, I like to be prepared. I checked out options online. I settled on a handy-dandy pocket siren.'

All is revealed. 'Remind me to keep my distance.'

'Only in parking lots after dark.' She chuckles.

Do I detect a hint of intrigue? Leaving me to wonder if there's a technique to making out while wearing a hand splint. There's nothing saying you have to be ambidextrous between the sheets.

Mae stays the night, and not solely out of sympathy for the injured man.

It has been a long (yes, on occasion, tedious) period of abstinence. There was more than enough happening to take my mind off it, fortunately, most of the time.

Let's just say it's worth the wait. No, let's smile broadly and say it's well worth the wait.

And yes, the splint proved to be no hindrance whatsoever.

The call comes out of the blue late the next morning. Mae is at work. I'm just back from walking Gaffer, having had limited success bagging dog poop while, with the one usable hand, also gripping the mutt's leash.

'Sebastian, how are you doing?'

Samantha. Surprise, surprise. Not only that, but in the middle of the day, while she's hard at it as school principal.

'Fine. You know me, I'm a good healer.'

'Thankfully no broken bones this time.'

I think I detect sincerity, not sarcasm. Do I also detect an overturned leaf?

'Are you free to come to dinner tomorrow night?'

A second, stiffer, jolt.

'Sure.' In the nick of time, before hesitation starts sounding like disbelief.

'I've already talked to Mae, she's fine with it.'

So either she asked Mae to run it by me and Mae suggested she ask me herself, or she planned to call me anyway.

No point going there. 'Great.'

'See you both around seven. And Sebastian, bring Gaffer if you like.'

I make an intense cup of coffee and drink it black.

Or, I'm thinking, Olsen pitched the idea and Samantha went along with it. In which case it may be the informal situation that Olsen needs to fill us in on what's happened without doing it in his official capacity as an RNC officer. In other words, keep his professional life clean while acknowledging that we deserve to be clued in, given that without Mae and me, the cops would be still back on Fogo Island barking up the wrong tree.

It's a very long wait to the time we arrive at the house, bottle of robust Shiraz in hand. I still find it strange to be ringing the doorbell of the house I occupied for a sizable chunk of my existence. But there it is. Life takes many paths.

I look at Mae and smile. This new path feels more stable than some I've taken.

Nick throws open the door. 'Come on in, you guys.' He's overdoing the welcome, but that's okay. Gaffer bypasses our legs and makes for him, as Samantha and Frederick emerge from the kitchen. Nothing like a dog to dispel tension.

'Hi, folks. Thanks for having us over.' I'm into it, somewhat cooler than cool.

'Good to see us all together again,' says Samantha.

Yes, definitely an overturned leaf. Given how the prior meeting of the minds had ended.

Frederick starts the motion to shake my hand, forgetting the splint, but quickly turns the open hand to a casual fist that jabs the air. 'No worse for wear. Good job.'

A bit tricky, but he pulled it off. 'Thanks.'

The opening act takes place in the living room over wine. There's a cheese and smoked meat platter, which I suspect was picked up from Sobeys on the way home from work.

I stop myself in mid-thought. Judgmental is not good. Samantha has a demanding job. Her kitchen time is limited. She wants this to work. The least I can do is show my appreciation. I top a second cracker with prosciutto and brie and consume it eagerly.

'I've ordered in dinner,' says Samantha. 'It'll be ready when we are.'

I'm biting my tongue. Instead I'm thinking it's all to the good, given what I've witnessed when Samantha's been cooking under pressure. Instead, we're all sitting together, semi-relaxed and waiting for someone to take the first step into the inevitable topic of conversation.

Ideally that would be Inspector Olsen. He's the man of the hour, surrounded by varying levels of anticipation. The conversation is waning. Interest in the pros and cons of turning fifty can only last so long before it wears itself out.

Leave it to Nick, who is obviously bored by it all, to jump in with both feet. 'So,' he says, 'who do you think killed the unfortunate woman?' He's perfectly serious, as if he's got every right to an answer.

Given his age and peripheral connection to the case, Nick, of everyone present, should be the least privy to inside information. He realizes this, of course. He's figuring he's got nothing to lose.

He glances in my direction. It dawns on me that he sees it as doing me a favour. Saving his old man the embarrassment of asking himself.

Olsen shifts his position in the armchair, ill at ease. Although willing to drum up an answer, it seems.

'This much I can tell you.' His boundaries are set.

Nevertheless, showing promise. I try upping his comfort level. 'What happens in Vegas stays in Vegas.'

Olsen shoots me a look that's hard to read exactly. He eventually makes eye contact with everyone else in the room.

'I'm telling you this because you might have something to add that could be useful.' Then he tentatively dives in. 'At this point we have three scenarios at play.'

Anyone expecting a definitive answer is disappointed. I, for one, am not. This case has never been cut and dried.

'Kaleb is telling us it was Rosalita. Who, as we discovered, is Octavia's cousin.'

'Which,' says Mae, 'made Gertie half-aunt to them both. And both therefore Gertie's half-nieces.'

This half business always gets to me.

'According to Kaleb,' says Olsen, 'a confrontation with Gertie over Rosalita's grandfather's will got out of hand.'

'You mean Gertie's father, the Puerto Rican soldier,' says Mae, 'also Octavia's grandfather.' Easy enough for her to figure out, she being the one who first suggested there might be family connections.

'On the other hand,' says Olsen, 'Rosalita swears it was Connie, because Kaleb was having an affair.'

No surprises there. But in my mind Rosalita has no credibility whatsoever.

'And then there's Connie, who says it was Kaleb, to keep Gertie from spilling the beans on their affair.'

That one I definitely don't buy. 'Kaleb is not the murdering type.'

A lead balloon. 'Gender bias,' counters Mae, saving Samantha the trouble.

'I'm sticking with Rosalita,' I tell them. 'My bet is on someone who came from elsewhere.'

It seems I have a knack for striking nerves. 'So,' says Samantha, 'what you're telling us is that no outport man would commit murder. It's not in his DNA.' She overstates it.

'No. What I am saying is that unless he's mentally unstable, which I see no evidence of, I very much doubt he would act so violently toward Gertie, especially if they liked each other enough to have an affair.'

'The man who held two people hostage with a shotgun,' inserts Olsen.

'We all know he was faking it. He let them go.'

'What about Connie?' says Mae, as gently as she can manage it. 'Outport woman. Also incapable of murder?'

'I would say Connie's ability to control her emotions is debatable. Under certain circumstances, maybe she'd go over the edge. Was her husband having an affair enough to do that? I doubt it. But if it was, it's more likely her rage would go straight to Kaleb.' A pause. 'I'm sticking with Rosalita.'

There's an uneasy lull in the conversation. Olsen is the one to break it. 'I should tell you this. Inspector Bowmore has been back and forth with the detachment on Fogo Island, getting them to dig deeper into Rosalita's background. They talked to some of her in-laws. It seems there were unanswered questions about her husband's death. He died of a heart attack, but an autopsy was never done to confirm what caused it. His relatives pointed out that he had no history of a heart condition and that he kept in pretty good shape. Two years ago he did the 10K event during the Fogo Island Race Weekend. Walked most of the way, but still.'

Need I say more? The evidence is piling high.

Olsen, however, is not about to assign guilt. It's not what cops do. That will eventually be the job of a jury.

It looks like we've reached a finishing line, for now. As unsatisfactory as that is.

A lengthy pause for wine and nibblies before Nick pipes up, 'So, folks, what say we have dinner. Everyone take a seat at the table. I'll handle the food.'

The lad has a gift for reading the crowd. Tensions ease as we get to our feet, wine glasses in hand. Conversations take new directions.

'Who thinks the Leafs have a chance at the Cup?' Nick adds for good measure.

Samantha and Mae seat themselves, commiserating, if you can believe it, over the need for a high-end "Nordic" spa just outside the city.

I had an experience with a spa once in Mexico. Not something I want to repeat.

'Thermal pools outdoors, overlooking the ocean,' says Samantha.

'Just imagine it,' says Mae, 'in a snow squall on the edge of the North Atlantic. They'd come from all over the world. If the Fogo Island Inn can do it . . .'

Meanwhile, back in the real world, Nick has started the retrieval of the Thai food from the oven, where it's been kept warm. He sets it out on the table one dish at a time. 'More wine anyone? Help yourselves.'

I must say we're turning into an affable lot, the five of us around the table. Who would have thought it? Not me, for one.

All good. Not that I need to be telling myself that.

'Cheers, everyone,' says Nick. He raises his water glass, clinks it against each of our wine glasses.

The young man is desperate to make this work. The last thing I'm about to do is stand in his way.

I see him slip a shrimp from his plate and let his hand drop between our chairs, to where Gaffer has been lying since we sat down. Not something his mother would approve of. But he knows he has an ally in me.

I'm very happy to have it stay that way.

GATHER TOGETHER

THE REST OF the week is taken up with much needed R and R—rest and recuperation. Mixed with planning for the tours coming up this summer. Much of the time it's just Gaffer and me and refreshments. Mae is on the scene, but intermittently. Time apart is good, I tell myself, because when we do get together it's all the more rewarding. In the spiritual, non-material sense of course.

Although she would never admit to it, Mae has been leading me to the benefits of pacing myself, of restraint. I'm a quick learner in most regards, although, to be honest, this particular life lesson has its challenges.

We talk on the phone quite a bit. If she's not actually present, her voice is never far away. And never too serious. Full of healthy good humour. Lots of give and take. And, surprisingly, not much about the investigation. I'm getting the sense she feels I need to be digesting it on my own, reinforcing my confidence as a PI, without her being part of the picture.

Let's just say I'm on the up and up in that regard and leave it at that.

'Guess who came in the shop today?' An unusual opening

line. None of her normal phone preliminaries. No hi, how are you, did you have a productive day?

'I dunno. A quilter who just won the lottery?'

'Octavia.'

Stunned. 'You're joking.' So much for keeping the investigation off the table.

'She had heard a lot about St. John's, so she decided that once she finished up on Fogo Island she'd take a few days to visit the city and fly home from here. Tomorrow is her last day.'

'So, did you guys talk long? What did she have to say?'

'Not much, really. The shop wasn't the place to have much of a conversation. But she did seem genuinely pleased to see me. She gave me a lovely hug.'

No surprise there.

'We set a time to meet tomorrow evening, for dinner.'

A little more stunned. 'That's great.' I don't ask the obvious question.

But Mae, of course, knows exactly what it is.

'She asked if I would invite you to come along.'

Really? I admit Octavia and I have had our issues. 'That's generous of her.'

'So you're good with that?'

'I'll hold back. It's you she wants to talk to.'

'Seven o'clock. At Terre in the Alt Hotel. And, Sebastian . . . just be yourself.'

I leave it at that. We'll just wait and see who I turn out to be.

The Alt is one of the newer, sleeker downtown hotels. Terre has an exceptional reputation. The view of St. John's harbour from the restaurant is not great. But no doubt much better from the pricier rooms.

I'm on edge. I shouldn't be, I know. Once I spot Mae, seated alone at a table, I get a grip. She's the first to arrive. She's sipping a cocktail.

The table is set for three. I take the seat next to her. 'Hi, what's up?'

My voice is not quite on target. Nothing slips by Mae, of course.

I turn attention to the bar menu. Mae is drinking what's called a Rhubarb Cosmos.

'Rhubarb vodka, cranberry juice (both local products), and Cointreau,' she says, adding, 'Have a Scotch. I know you're not into cocktails.'

She's right there. As much as I like to support local.

The Scotch choices are good. And they do have Talisker.

There's no chance for the whisky to blunt the nerves before Mae catches sight of Octavia entering the restaurant. She waves to her. Mae stands up and circles the table to welcome her with a hug. I'm on my feet as well, partly out of politeness, partly out of the need for her to see why I'm incapable of a handshake.

What she's wearing is more subdued than what we had come to expect. Only her shoulder bag is quilted. Once she's settled in the chair across the table, the focus is her cable-knit cardigan, in a colour that Mae calls 'periwinkle blue.'

'I bought it at Nonia,' Octavia tells her. 'I couldn't resist.'

The legendary knitwear shop on Water Street. A Newfoundland institution for a hundred years. The sweater would be a bit warm for Brooklyn this time of year, I expect, but perfect for spring in Newfoundland.

'What happened to your hand?' she asks, after ordering a glass of white wine.

'It's a long story.' And not one I particularly want to tell. Not a great prelude to dinner, but, then again, better over drinks than over beef tartare.

I do my best to avoid mentioning Rosalita specifically as the one responsible, but it comes to the point where it's obvious.

'I saw her this afternoon,' Octavia asserts.

I'm surprised. Not so much by what she said as how overtly she volunteered the information. Both Mae and I had been wondering, of course, if Octavia would attempt to make contact with her cousin while in the city, given all that's happened between them.

She would have seen Rosalita behind bars.

'What was she saying?' The obvious question, but one that can only sound blunt.

'That she's innocent.'

'Do you believe her?' The frankness continues, on both sides of the table.

'Rosie's had a tough several years,' she says. 'She survived an abusive marriage but never did get any sympathy from her grandfather, who she thought could have helped to restart her life. When he died and it came out whom he had left his money to, her anger got the best of her.'

I can't think she's intentionally making excuses for Rosalita.

'So she set out to find Gertie?' Mae says.

'It took a while, by which time Gertie had spent some of the money to set up her shop. Some, but not all. There would have been quite a bit left.'

'She ended up on Change Islands married to Jack Tizzard,' I say. 'That's the part I don't get—how she managed that.'

'Online dating.'

'Really?'

'That's what I gather. I imagine she made the rounds of quite a few sites before she finally found a profile that fit what she was looking for. Maybe she was hoping for Fogo Island itself, but in the end Change Islands was a better fit.'

'She could observe from a distance, before choosing a time to confront Gertie.'

'I would think that over the year since she came to Change

Islands she went to the shop several times,' Octavia says. 'She would have seen how comfortable Gertie was and how much she was loved by people who knew her. It must have left Rosie thinking it could have been her, had she received some of her grandfather's inheritance.'

'Do you really think so?' asks Mae. 'Gertie would have still been happy if the inheritance had never come along. She was a good person to begin with.'

Octavia looks intently at both Mae and me. 'And we are all thinking Rosie was not?'

There's a prolonged silence.

'I never did know her to be happy, except when we played together as kids. As an adult her life took a turn she never recovered from. She grew bitter. Gertie, unfortunately, became the focus of that bitterness.'

It leaves me doubtful if it's as simple as that. I recall people who overcame adversity and put their lives back together.

'Few people know this,' says Octavia, 'but I'll tell you. Rosie always wanted a child, but she never could conceive. There was a reason, a medical one, but it made it no easier. I think she believed a child would help solve her marital problems. Even when the marriage was over and she tried to adopt, it never worked out. She was not considered stable enough to raise a child. It broke her heart.'

Hardly a reason to murder someone. Octavia, I can tell, is reading my mind.

'I don't believe she went in that shop with the intention of killing Gertie. I honestly don't. Something was triggered that she didn't control.' She looks at Mae. 'Maybe it was that picture you showed me, the one on Gertie's desk, of our Papi and Gertie's mother?'

Mae is slow to respond. She might agree but she looks unwilling to commit to it. I feel the same way. A trigger, but undoubtedly no excuse to wield that pair of scissors.

'We'll never know,' says Octavia.

That may well be the case.

The food has started to arrive. It's a welcome opportunity to change the conversation.

For appetizers we seem to be on a seafood theme. There are rave reviews for the scallops and the mussels.

And as for what's in front of me, I've yet to tackle it. I'm too busy taking a photo to send to Nick, with the caption: *–getting one step ahead of impotence, constipation, frequent urination . . . and I forget the fourth.*

'Sea cucumber,' says Mae, wincing slightly. 'Better you than me.'

'*Braised* sea cucumber,' I point out. 'I couldn't resist.'

'Why aren't you eating it then?'

'I'm building up to it.'

'In Alabama I've eaten deep-fried dill pickles,' Octavia tells us, thinking it might stiffen my resolve.

I smile, then take the plunge.

Actually, it's not bad. A bit on the gelatinous side, but kind of interesting with the mushroom and oyster garlic sauce.

I check my phone.

–joint pain, says Nick. *any leftovers bring a doggie bag*

Right. Four medicinal bases covered. I consume it all, sop up the remaining sauce with a fresh roll, and feel very good about myself.

The remainder of the evening is all about the food. Well, food and fabric.

Fabric art to be more precise. Octavia's talk went very well. As did her exhibition. A number of pieces sold.

'Congratulations.' I mean that sincerely. My appreciation of fabric art has taken a giant leap forward.

'I have something for you, Sebastian.'

Really. I wasn't expecting that. If it's a gift, it should be for Mae.

'I sometimes take a single word and use it as catalyst for a small piece that can be mounted on five-by-seven cardstock. Just a little something to remember our interaction.'

Octavia withdraws an envelope from her quilted bag and passes it across the table to me.

I'm a bit embarrassed, to be honest. I'd be the first to admit that I wasn't totally understanding of her.

They're both waiting for me to open it. I remove the card from its envelope.

Several small pieces of different fabrics have been assembled and stitched together in a colourful, irregular composition. There's a vague almond shape that somewhat resembles an open eye. Just below the piece and to the left Octavia has hand-written the title—'Objectivity.' To the right is her signature.

Yes, objectivity is the point, people. No comment.

'Thank you, Octavia. Thank you very much. It's very kind.'

'No expectations,' she says. 'Put it away if it doesn't appeal to you.'

'Or you could frame it,' says Mae. 'It would look lovely on an end table.'

Let's wait and see. On an end table it would be competing with a dram of Scotch.

In the meantime there's dessert to consider. Which for me has to be the Alder Sugar Beignets, with whiskey sauce. Even though I prefer my whisky without an 'e' and I have no clue what beignets are.

'French,' Mae informs me. 'Deep-fried dough really.'

'New Orleans is famous for them,' says Octavia.

That would explain the 'e' in whiskey. 'You mean as opposed to Newfoundland fried dough.'

'Toutens,' Octavia declares, her accent adding a new charm

to the word. 'I love them. I'd come back to Newfoundland just for the toutens.'

Looking at it objectively, I believe she would.

Our time together is drawing to an end. Octavia has an early morning flight and some packing still to do.

We depart the restaurant and walk together to the elevator that will take her to her room.

'Please come back. There's so much more of Newfoundland and Labrador for you to experience,' I say to her. 'So much more to inspire you.'

I won't be saying this, but Octavia may have no choice but to come back—to testify.

'We'll see,' she tells us. 'No promises, but we'll see.' The panel above the elevator is about to end its countdown.

'We'll keep in touch,' says Mae. 'In the meantime . . .' she announces, spreading her arms wide. 'Group hug!'

ALSO IN THIS SERIES

One for the Rock
Two for the Tablelands
Three for Trinity

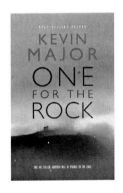

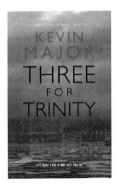